Corinne

By Wendy Wan-Long Shang
Illustrated by Peijin Yang

★ AmericanGirl®

Published by American Girl Publishing

22 23 24 25 26 27 28 QP 10 9 8 7 6 5 4 3 2 1

This book is a work of fiction. Any similarity to real persons, living or dead,
is coincidental and not intended by American Girl. References to real events,
people, or places are used fictitiously. Other names, characters, places,
and incidents are the products of imagination.

Illustrations by Peijin Yang
Cover image by Peijin Yang · Book design by Gretchen Becker

The following individuals and organizations have generously granted permission
to reproduce their photographs: pp. 130–133—Courtesy of Charlie Zelenak; p. 132—
Courtesy of Christy Pelland; p. 131—Courtesy of Ryan French. All rights reserved.

Cataloging-in-Publication Data available from the Library of Congress

americangirl.com/service

Not all services are available in all countries.

Dedicated to the girls who keep their faces to the sun.
—W.S.

Mom, Arne, Corinne, Gwynn

Corinne, Gwynn, Cassidy

Flurry

Corinne, Gwynn, Dad

With gratitude to:

Greta Gessele, professional figure skating instructor in Aspen. Greta started skating at age six and grew up competing and performing with the Aspen Skating Club.

Dr. Jennifer Ho, professor of ethnic studies at the University of Colorado Boulder, and president of the Association for Asian American Studies (2020–2022).

Angela Liu, digital marketing manager at American Girl and member of American Girl's diversity task force.

Lori Spence, director, Aspen Highlands Ski Patrol and avalanche dog trainer. Lori currently works with a black Labrador retriever named Meka.

Dr. William Wei, professor of modern Chinese history at the University of Colorado Boulder, and 2019–2020 Colorado State Historian.

Contents

Sister Brain

Chapter 1

*T*hree really excellent sounds go with skiing: the click of my boots in the bindings, the rhythmic whoosh of skis over snow, and the spray of a good hockey stop. There's nothing more relaxing than crisscrossing down the slope, admiring the trees, and enjoying a crisp breeze against my face.

"*Jie jie!*"—big sister—"Hurry up!"

One less-than-excellent sound also goes with skiing, and that is the voice of your little sister telling you to hurry up. I could pretend that I didn't hear her, but then Mom would get mad at me for not keeping closer to her. Instead I pointed my skis down the hill and caught up with Gwynn.

"Why are you going so slow?" she demanded.

"I wanted to look at the search and rescue dogs some more," I said. When we had gotten off the ski lift, a ski patrol team had been practicing finding people in the snow. Whenever a dog found someone, everyone cheered and made a big fuss, which made the dogs seem really proud of themselves. "Did you see that they had their own special harnesses?"

"I wonder if they like the harnesses," said Gwynn. "Maybe they feel like life jackets." Gwynn did not like wearing a life jacket when our family canoed in the summer. She said it felt like she was trapped inside a marshmallow.

"Maybe the harnesses make them feel like part of the team," I said. The dogs wore black harnesses with orange accents, which matched the ski patrollers' jackets.

"Maybe the harnesses make them feel fancy," said Gwynn. She was looking at her ski jacket, which was decidedly not fancy. It was my hand-me-down, which had been passed down to me from one of Mom's coworkers' kids.

At the bottom of the hill, I saw Mom looking for us. We were running late. "Mom's waiting. We should get going."

Gwynn put her mittened hand inside mine. "Cori, are you nervous?"

I was nervous. But I didn't want Gwynn to be nervous, too. "I won't be after I beat you to the bottom," I said. I pulled my goggles down. "Race you!"

"Hey, wait! No fair!" cried Gwynn. But she was laughing. We had skied our worries away, at least for a few moments.

🌲🌲🌲

Sister Brain

It was Mom's idea for us to walk to Arne's house from the ski slope. She wanted us to see how cool it would be to live there. Arne is Mom's fiancé. Fiancé means the person you're going to marry, though Gwynn called Arne Mom's "fancy" for a long time, so Mom and I called him that, too. Gwynn also said his name "Army," until Mom taught her to say "Arr-nee." Arne had been to our house many times, but Gwynn and I had visited his house only a couple of times. Mom said that was because our house was more "kid-friendly." But now that they were getting married, we'd be moving into Arne's house because it's bigger.

We put our skis and poles on the ski racks outside, and then Mom let us in. Arne wasn't home, but Mom had a key.

"I remember watching *Matilda* here," said Gwynn, pointing. "Arne fell asleep in that chair. He kept saying, '*Springa springa springa!*'" That meant "run" in Swedish, Arne's first language.

I smiled at the memory of Arne stretched out in the chair with his mouth open. "You talk in your sleep, too," I reminded Gwynn. At home, she and I shared a room, and sometimes she said things when she was sound asleep. "Last night you said you needed feathers for our spaghetti, and when I asked you why, you said, 'Balloons!'"

Gwynn nodded. "I was dreaming about flying," she said.

Today, we got to go upstairs in Arne's house for the first

time. We climbed up one flight of stairs, past the kitchen and living room, and then up one more flight. Mom said that there were enough bedrooms that Gwynn and I could each have our own. Even though I was nervous about moving, I was excited to have a room just for me.

Mom opened the doors to our rooms. "Ta-da!" she said. "You even get your own bathrooms." The rooms were bigger than the one that Gwynn and I shared at home, but they didn't look like they were for kids. They looked like hotel rooms—pretty, but boring.

Mom saw my face. "When you move your stuff in, it will feel more like your room," she promised. "Right now, these are guest bedrooms."

"Where's your room?" Gwynn asked Mom. Arne's house was a town house, which meant that every floor only had a few rooms, but there were more floors to spread them out. There were only two rooms on this floor.

"Upstairs," said Mom. "The master bedroom takes up the whole top floor. Do you want to see?" We nodded and followed her upstairs. The room was full of windows so you could see the mountains as well as downtown Aspen. There was a big bed with soft, velvety bedding, and a fireplace with a television and a comfy couch in front of it. "That's Arne's closet," Mom said pointing to one door. "And that will be my closet. And that's the bathroom."

"You could just live up here!" I said. There was even a little refrigerator tucked off to one side.

"That doesn't sound too terrible," said Mom, teasing. "We could have a movie night up here. Wouldn't that be fun?" She started to say more, but her phone rang. "Let me take this," she said. "I think it's about the restaurant." Mom was working on opening a restaurant that sells different kinds of Chinese street food—traditional dishes from China that people could buy at a counter. The space was really small, so it was mostly for takeout, not eating in.

While Mom was on the phone, Gwynn's lower lip began to poke out, which was a sign that she was unhappy. "If I have a nightmare, I'll have to come all the way up the stairs in the dark to find Mom," she said. At home, Mom's bedroom was right next to ours.

"Oh," I said, thinking quickly. "You haven't had a nightmare in a long time. I think you've outgrown them."

"Or what if I get sick?" asked Gwynn. "And she can't hear me because she's all the way upstairs?"

I didn't want Gwynn to worry. Moving was weird and hard, even though Arne's house was so nice. Or maybe *because* Arne's house was so nice.

I put my hand in Gwynn's. "I was thinking," I said, "that it would be nice if we still shared a room. These rooms seem too big for one person."

Gwynn gasped. "That's what I was thinking!" She paused. "We must be having sister brain," she said solemnly.

Gwynn liked to think that we could communicate without talking. She called it sister brain. I didn't think we could actually communicate that way. Most of the time, it was obvious we both felt the same way, like when we both got bored on a long car ride. But I pretended along with her.

"Yup," I said. "That's exactly right."

"Do you think Arne will let us paint our room purple?" asked Gwynn. She lingered on the word *our,* savoring it. We had one purple wall in our room at home. Mom had let us choose the color. We'd picked a bright shade that reminded us of the columbine flowers we saw in the spring.

"I'm sure he will," I said. "Mom did, didn't she?"

Mom finished her phone call. She must have heard some of what we were saying, because when Gwynn wasn't looking, she caught my eye and mouthed *Thank you* for keeping Gwynn happy.

🌲🌲

Mom made dinner in Arne's kitchen while Gwynn and I worked on homework at the table. Gwynn was lucky. Being seven, she had easy homework, like reading for twenty minutes. My fifth-grade homework was harder. Today I had math problems plus a worksheet about the

Indigenous people of Colorado. I picked up every little scrap of eraser dust when I had to change one of my answers, because Arne's house was so clean.

Mom watched me carefully carry the dust to the trash can. "I wish you were this neat at home," she said. Then she corrected herself. "This is also going to be our home, so I'm glad you're cleaning up after yourself, Corinne."

"The house is so clean, it makes me nervous," I said. "I'm afraid to mess anything up." At our house, we had toys on the floor and artwork by Gwynn and me on the walls. It was hard to imagine how our things would fit in Arne's house, even if we had our own bedroom.

"It's important to be tidy, but it's also important to be comfortable," said Mom. "We'll find a way." She was roasting peanuts to go with the sesame noodle dish she was cooking.

Gwynn poked me. "Sister brain says you're hungry."

"Sister brain says it's getting close to dinnertime," I said. "And who wouldn't be hungry when Mom's cooking?"

A Purple-Colored Wish

Chapter 2

A door opened and closed. Arne came in carrying his laptop case and some shopping bags. "Hey, hey!" said Arne. "Has my house been invaded? Am I Goldilocks? I am certainly wanting some of this wonderful porridge!" Arne grew up in Sweden. He speaks English very well, though sometimes his words come out a little choppy.

Mom laughed. "If you want porridge, then I guess I'll throw away these sesame noodles," she teased.

"Ah! No, no! Goldilocks is very happy with sesame noodles." Arne calls himself Goldilocks as a joke, because his hair is so light and blond compared with our dark hair. I think he's trying to connect with us, because it's a children's story. He doesn't seem to know we're too old for Goldilocks. He put his arm around Mom and tried to sneak a bite of sesame noodles.

Mom and Arne met when Mom was catering a party. The way Mom told the story, after Arne tasted her food, he spent the rest of the party in the kitchen with her instead of with the other guests. Arne's version of the story was that Mom kept giving him extra-small portions so he would have to come ask for more.

"Well, what do you girls think of your new bedrooms?" he asked, smiling. "Did you each pick one out?"

"We're going to share a room, just like we do now," said Gwynn.

"Oh?" Arne looked disappointed. "But there is so much room here! You do not need to share." He waved his arms around. "You can spread out."

"We don't *need* to, but we *want* to," I explained. "It's what we're used to." I didn't want to talk about Gwynn's worries in front of Arne, so I hoped that would be enough explanation. "But we would like to paint one of the walls purple."

"Purple?" Arne sounded surprised. "*Purple?*" He looked around the room, which was painted in shades of beige and white. No purple.

"You know," said Mom, "like the girls' bedroom now."

Arne sighed. "Purple. Let me think about it," he said.

"Let's think over dinner," said Mom. She lifted the pan from the stove and carried it to the table.

Arne tapped his stomach. "*That* is a very good idea."

He said *that* as if the noodles were a good idea, but a purple bedroom was a terrible idea. A knot tightened in my stomach. Would Arne get to decide everything once we lived together?

Over dinner, Arne and Mom talked about the wedding. They planned to go to city hall and then have dinner out with friends. Mom, Gwynn, and I had picked out new dresses, all in shades of red, and Arne would wear his favorite suit.

"It's who you marry, not how you marry," said Arne.

"I still wish you were going to have the kind of wedding where I could be a flower girl," said Gwynn.

"It's *their* wedding," I told her. I was actually a little relieved that they weren't having a wedding with lots of people. I was glad that Mom was happy, and I liked Arne. But I was still sad that my parents were not together, and I worried how Dad felt about us moving in with Arne. A small wedding made all those feelings more manageable because it was quiet and private, not big and out in the open.

"You can still be a flower girl," Arne told Gwynn. "You hold flowers, like Mommy, okay? I will order a bouquet for you. Do you want one, too, Corinne?"

I had never had a bouquet of flowers before—not one of my very own. "Yes, please," I said.

"After the wedding, we'll go away for one night while you two are with Dad," said Mom. "And then we will officially move in here."

A Purple-Colored Wish

"Is Daddy coming to the wedding?" asked Gwynn.

"No! Don't be silly," I said. "That's not what happens after people get divorced."

"I thought Mom and Dad would both be at important things," said Gwynn.

That's what Mom and Dad always told us. When we had school plays or back-to-school night, Mom and Dad both came, and they both took us trick-or-treating.

"This is different," said Mom. "And Daddy understands. We talked about it." She put her hand on top of Gwynn's and looked at Arne. "Maybe this is a good time to share the surprise."

"Ah yes! Surprise! Who likes surprises?" Arne rubbed his hands together and grinned at Gwynn and me. "So, is there a certain young lady here who likes ice skating?"

"Me!" shouted Gwynn.

"We know you'd like to take private lessons," said Mom.

"So we've signed you up with your own instructor, Ms. Margot. Your first lesson is tomorrow," said Arne. He was smiling like a little kid.

Gwynn squealed. "Really? Really, really?"

This was my little sister's dream come true. Whenever we went to the rink, Gwynn always watched the skaters in the middle wistfully. She had taken group lessons, but private coaches cost more money.

Corinne

My stomach sank for a moment, even though I loved seeing Gwynn so happy. Cassidy, my best friend, didn't like girls who took private skating lessons. She thought they were snobs. I think her feelings came from one bad experience she had with a skater at the rink last year, which isn't really fair. Just because one girl was rude to her didn't mean that all skaters were snobs. Gwynn definitely wasn't. I hoped Cassidy wouldn't hold these private lessons against Gwynn—or against me.

Arne brought over a shopping bag. "And of course, you must also have a new outfit." He held up a pair of leggings, a top, and a matching fleece headband. The tags were still on them. Gwynn's eyes widened. New clothes were a rare treat.

Gwynn jumped out of her chair. "This is the best day ever!" she cried. She ran over to Arne and gave him a hug and then hugged Mom. "I'm going to practice skating every single day!" All the difficult parts of our day were forgotten. Gwynn danced in a circle, waving around her new outfit.

"That's what I like to hear," said Arne. "That is the attitude of a champion." He turned to me. "I wanted to do the same for you, Corinne. Maybe skiing lessons?"

"I don't want to ski like that," I said, trying to say it politely. "Not in competitions. I just ski for fun because I like being outside, out on the mountain."

A Purple-Colored Wish

"That's what I suspected," said Mom. She gave Arne a knowing look. "And that's fine, Corinne. It's fine to ski for fun. And Dad can teach you whatever you need to know."

My dad is a ski instructor in Aspen. Because he also speaks Mandarin and Spanish, his specialty is teaching people whose first language is not English.

"But it's good to have a special skill to master," said Arne. "You think of something, okay? I want to treat you girls fairly."

"Okay," I said, though I really couldn't think of anything. The knot in my stomach got bigger. Would Arne still like me if I didn't have a "special skill" like Gwynn? What if I just wanted to be me?

Slap in the Face
Chapter 3

*T*he next day, we all went to the skating rink to watch Gwynn's first lesson. Her new practice outfit looked so pretty. Pink ribbons accented the dark blue leggings, and the pale blue top matched her headband. Gwynn was so excited that she kept jumping up and down in her skates on the rubber mat and announcing facts she had learned from Ms. Margot's website. "Ms. Margot (hop hop) got a silver medal at regionals when she was seventeen." "Ms. Margot (hop hop) also likes hiking and baking." When she finally got to meet Ms. Margot, Gwynn couldn't stop smiling. They chatted for a few minutes, and then Gwynn did a few warm-up laps around the rink to show her skills.

Arne walked to the snack bar for a cup of coffee, and Mom turned to me. "I wanted to talk to you about the purple wall," she said quietly. "I know you're disappointed Arne didn't agree to it right away, but the house is professionally decorated. He's not used to, you know, painting a wall whatever color he wants. He needs to talk to his decorator and see what she thinks."

"Okay," I said. But inside I had a million questions spinning around. What else was going to be different about living with Arne? Would he get mad if we made a mess? Would he need to ask his decorator about my purple bed-spread? Maybe he wouldn't want us to have movie night in the master bedroom because it was *his* room.

"We'll work it out," said Mom, rubbing my arm. "Don't worry. And, Corinne, I really do appreciate the fact that you offered to share a room with Gwynn. I think that will be a big help for her. And who knows? Maybe down the road you two will want separate rooms."

I wished Mom could see all the questions inside me so I wouldn't need to say them out loud. I nodded and watched Gwynn on the ice. Ms. Margot was helping her turn on one foot and skate backward. Gwynn looked a little wobbly, but she was smiling. They came over to our side of the rink just as Arne returned with his coffee.

"I'm so excited to work with this young lady!" said Ms. Margot. "She's going to have her half flip in no time." The coach had a bright smile and rosy cheeks. "She tells me she wants to be the next Alysa Liu." Alysa Liu was Gwynn's idol. She was the youngest US national skating champion ever.

"We're in favor of that!" said Mom. She put her arm around Gwynn.

Corinne

"Now, I typically don't push my students to do a competition so quickly, but there's one coming up next month that I think would be perfect for her. What do you think? Should we try?" asked Ms. Margot.

"Yes," said Gwynn. "Please? Can I do it?" She clapped her hands, but she was wearing mittens, so the result was a series of muffled *whumps.*

"Of course," said Arne. "Gwynn Tan, our little champion! Just tell us what to do, Ms. Margot."

Arne and the teacher began talking about dates and schedules, while Mom took Gwynn to change in the locker room. "We'll meet you out in the car," Mom told us.

Arne and I walked around the rink to the exit. Arne stopped to throw away his coffee cup, so I went through the doors first, just as two older boys were coming in.

"Don't touch that door," said the shorter boy. He was wearing a blue plaid shirt and had jagged bangs that hung over his face like icicles. He knocked his friend's hand down. "*She* just touched it." *She* was me.

"What are you talking about?" said the other boy.

"Her!" The boy with jagged bangs pointed at me. "She has coronavirus! Kung flu!"

The taller boy started laughing. He pulled his sleeve over his hand so he didn't have to touch the door.

I couldn't have been more surprised if the boy had

slapped me. I stood there, just outside the doors, and watched them walk into the ice arena.

Arne came outside. "Do you remember where the car is?" he asked. He hadn't heard.

"One of those boys just said I had coronavirus," I said. "He called it *kung flu*." I felt like crying. I didn't have coronavirus. I didn't even know that boy. But it still hurt.

"What?" said Arne. "You must have misheard, Corinne. Don't cry. Maybe he has an accent like me." He put his arm around me. "People like that don't live here, honey."

I knew what I had heard, but Arne almost had me convinced. Maybe they had been teasing me. But more than the words, the boy's tone was what had struck me the hardest. It was mean, it was sharp, and it wasn't meant to be kind. I didn't know how to tell Arne that part so he would believe me.

"Hey," said Arne. "I wanted to do something for you, so I have linked my credit card account to your ski pass. You can use it to buy food or whatnot."

I wasn't sure how to take this news. "Thank you," I said. "Um, my mom usually gives me money for days when I need lunch. Or I have to pack something."

"Yah, yah. And then there are days you just want a snack. Or maybe you need new gloves or something. Now you don't worry whether you have money or not." Arne smiled. "I trust you to be reasonable."

When Arne said that, I felt really grown up. It was nice to be trusted like that.

"If you can eat after riding in that thing—the gondola," added Arne. He pointed upward and shook his head. "My stomach would get so churned up, I could not eat."

"You don't like the gondola?" I asked.

One of the amazing things about Aspen is how easy it is to go skiing. Four ski resorts surround Aspen. There's a ski lift right by my school. A gondola is a lift that takes you up the mountain in an enclosed car, and one starts right in downtown Aspen. It's called the Silver Queen.

"I am, how do you say it, acro . . . acrophobotic," Arne said. "No, wait. That's not right. Fear of heights. That is easier to say."

"Oh," I said. "I think it's called acrophobia." It was kind of funny to think that Arne was afraid of something I wasn't, but I also liked that he admitted to being scared. "It's okay, we all have things we're afraid of." I thought of the boy with the bangs.

Slap in the Face

We waited in the car until Mom and Gwynn came out.

"Gwynn can't wait for her next lesson!" said Mom as she climbed into the passenger seat. "I'd say that was a success."

"Wonderful," said Arne. He looked back at me in the rearview mirror. "Corinne and I also had a good chat, yes, Corinne?" He was talking about the ski pass. Everyone was in such a good mood that I decided not to mention the boys and kung flu. Maybe Arne had already forgotten.

Busman's Holiday

Chapter 4

*T*he next day, Dad came to pick up Gwynn and me for our weekend together. We had been packing boxes to get ready to move to Arne's house.

"Wow," Dad said, looking around. "It's the end of an era."

I ran to give him a hug and wondered if he was feeling sad. We all used to live in this house, until my parents got divorced. Now my dad lived farther away, in Basalt. Gwynn gave him a hug, too.

"Should the girls stay to help some more?" he asked Mom. "Looks like you still have a lot to do."

"No, no," said Mom. "It's your time with them. And they worked hard." She paused. "But maybe you could drop off some boxes for me at the thrift shop, if it's on your way?"

Dad said he would. My parents don't know it, but seeing them talk nicely to each other makes me really happy, even if it's about dumb stuff. Or maybe especially when it's about dumb stuff. I remember when they used to fight about little things, like what kind of peanut butter we bought.

Busman's Holiday

In the car, Gwynn asked where we were going.

Dad put his arms up in the air. *"Bai tuo nai!"* he said. Dad spoke Chinese to us more often than Mom did, and sometimes he called us by our Chinese names—Mei-Ling for me, and Guang for Gwynn. It took me a second, but I figured out what he was saying. *Nai* is a word for milk, as in *niu nai*, cow's milk. *Bai tuo* sounded like butter.

"We're going skiing at Buttermilk!" I shouted. That was the ski resort where he worked.

Going to Buttermilk with my dad is probably the closest I'll ever get to hanging out with a celebrity. He's been teaching there forever, so everyone knows him and treats him like a king. He's also a really good ski instructor. Lots of people ask for him again and again or pass his name on to friends. During the winter, Dad has to work all the time, so getting a weekend with him is very, very special. He makes it up to us in the summer, but we know how important it is for him to work. When the resorts closed because of the coronavirus pandemic, Dad couldn't make any money.

When we got to Buttermilk, there was a crowd at the base. Every once in a while, we heard a long *oooooh!* and then clapping. We went to investigate. "Must be someone laying it down on X Park," said Dad. "Let's go see."

Sure enough, a single person was skiing down the slopestyle course, which is a series of rails and ramps for performing tricks. The skier glided backward, turned slightly and landed neatly on a railing, spun around while going down it, and then flew off, still going backward.

"Who," I asked, "is that?!"

"It's a ski fairy," said Gwynn, which wasn't wrong. Whoever it was, the mystery skier was light and graceful.

"Let me find out," said Dad. He stepped away to talk to some people who worked there. "It's Eileen Gu," he said when he came back. From the way he said her name, I knew she was important. "One of the best freeskiers around. She won her first World Cup when she was fifteen."

We watched Eileen ski some more. A man standing near us named some of the tricks as she performed them. Frontside four-fifty double-Japan. Alley-oop. Right-side cork nine hundred.

"Those names are funny," said Gwynn. "I'd call that one a curly fry with special sauce." She pointed as Eileen spun tightly in the air.

"She's amazing," I said. "She makes it look so easy."

"Don't be fooled, Corinne," said Dad. "She has a gift for it, but she also works really hard." Eileen reached the bottom of the hill and lifted up her goggles. She looked a little like my cousin, Millie. "Is she Chinese?" I asked. "Like us?"

"Her mom is Chinese," said Dad. "Her Chinese name is Gu Ailing." Ailing sounded like Eileen.

Busman's Holiday

"Until now, you were the most famous Chinese skier we knew," I said, teasing Dad.

"Can you teach us to ski like that?" asked Gwynn.

"I can teach you the basics," said Dad. "Let's go!"

🌲

Dad said that we had to learn how to ski switch before we learned any tricks. Skiing switch is a fancy way of saying skiing backward. He took us to an area that wasn't steep or crowded. Gwynn tried first, but she kept stopping every few feet.

"I don't like not being able to see all the way behind me," she said. "I'm afraid I'm going to run into someone."

"If people see you skiing backward, they're probably going to stay out of your way," said Dad.

"You try it," Gwynn said to me.

I tried to remember everything Dad showed us. Our skis were supposed to be shoulder-width apart and parallel. We were supposed to look over one shoulder while we went backward and bent our knees.

"How does Eileen Gu make this look so easy?" I grumbled when my skis crossed over each other, bringing me to a halt.

"Practice, practice, practice," said Dad. "Keep your feet staggered."

Corinne

I bent my knees and shifted so that my left ski was farther down the hill than my right ski. I gave a little push and focused on keeping my skis parallel. I went down the hill, farther and faster than Gwynn had gone.

"You're doing great!" called Dad. "Keep going! Roll your knee to the edge to turn." I tried and turned slightly, though I felt clumsy and slow. "This feels like doing something that I can already do, but the hard way," I said.

"When you have the basics down, building skills on top of them is easier," Dad said.

I nodded and tried again. It felt a tiny bit easier. Then a flash of color caught my eye.

"What's that?" I turned around so I could ski facing forward. Several aspen trees, which had smooth, white bark, seemed to have bands of color on them. We took off our skis and walked over to get a closer look. The trees were covered in comic strips!

I'd heard about shrines on the mountains around Aspen. In many places, shrines were religious, but here locals made them in honor of pretty much anything they wanted to celebrate. No one wrote down where they were, though. You had to know or know someone who knew.

Gwynn studied the comic strips, which were sealed in plastic. "The little boy seems kind of naughty," she said. "Look at all these faces he's making!"

Busman's Holiday

"That was part of his charm. Calvin and Hobbes was a popular comic strip when I was little," explained Dad. "Calvin is a boy, and Hobbes is his stuffed tiger who can talk."

"Why would someone make a shrine about a comic strip?" I asked.

"Someone must have really liked Calvin and Hobbes," said Dad. He shrugged. "You like what you like. It's a special day when you find a shrine!"

"Even more special when you have a skiing lesson with your favorite teacher," I said.

"Today is a busman's holiday," said Dad.

"What's that?" I asked.

"A busman's holiday is when you do the same thing for fun that you do for work," said Dad. "I'm a lucky guy."

"If Arne had a busman's holiday," said Gwynn, "he would spend it on the phone and going to meetings."

I gave Gwynn a nudge. "You shouldn't talk about Arne in front of Dad."

Gwynn's lip quivered. "I didn't mean anything."

"Of course you didn't," said Dad. "It's not a big deal. You can talk about Arne." Even though Dad acted as if he meant it, I didn't quite believe him. If Dad got a new kid in his life, I would feel jealous. I thought Dad would feel the same way if I got a new dad in my life.

Corinne

At the end of the day, we went to Dad's house. For a moment as we were leaving the resort, I got confused about why we were heading away from town. Then I remembered that we weren't going home-home. I'd always thought of the house that Mom, Gwynn, and I lived in as our home. Now our choices were going to be Arne's house or Dad's house. I didn't call either place home.

There was a note on the door at Dad's house.

"What does it say?" I asked.

Dad took it down before I could read it. "Management is reminding us to be careful about throwing away food. Some bears got into the dumpsters," said Dad. He shook his head. "Bears can be dangerous. My friend Alex survived a bear attack. He lost his left thumb and has scars up and down his arm."

"I thought bears hibernated in the winter," said Gwynn.

"They're supposed to," said Dad. "But sometimes they'll skip hibernating if they have a steady food source. I guess that's what happened here." He looked at Gwynn and me. "You know that if you see a black bear, you don't try to outrun it. Bears are fast. You make yourself as big and loud as possible and try to scare it away."

Busman's Holiday

"I don't even know where the dumpster is," I said.

"Let's keep it that way for now," said Dad. "I don't want you girls accidentally running into a bear."

Keeping Secrets
Chapter 5

I couldn't figure out how to tell my best friend, Cassidy, about Arne. She knew that my mom was getting remarried to a guy named Arne, and she had even seen him once when Mom and Arne picked me up at a birthday party. But she didn't really *know* Arne. She didn't know where he lived—or that he was rich. Cassidy had a lot of opinions about things, including people like Arne who live in town. She called the people who lived in town *those people. Those people get new cars every year,* she'd say, while her mom was driving a ten-year-old Toyota. *Those people make normal birthdays seem boring,* she said, when we found out a girl at our school had a cowboy-themed birthday party, complete with horses and a rodeo. The snobby girl at the skating rink who was rude to Cassidy last year was one of *those people.*

I used to go along with Cassidy's opinion, but now things were different. I was about to start living with Arne. I knew Arne was not stuck-up. But what if Cassidy still thought I was becoming one of *those people*?

So when Cassidy met me at my locker, I only talked about going to Buttermilk with Dad and watching the slopestyle skiers. "We saw Eileen Gu!" I said. "She was amazing."

"Lucky," said Cassidy. "I had to help my mom clean the basement." She pouted and spun the dial on the locker next to mine. "But now our basement looks really nice, and Mom says you can come over for a sleepover. Maybe next Friday? It can't be this Friday because my grandma is coming to visit."

"Um," I said. "My mom is getting married that day." Normally I don't keep track of days very well, but that day was definitely on my mind. It was the first time I'd said anything about the wedding actually happening. It felt kind of weird.

"Really?" Cassidy's face lit up. "That's so cool! Can I come? I have a really nice dress to wear. And I could make us flower crowns to match the blue in your hair. It would look awesome!" Cassidy can make practically anything with her hands. Her best invention so far has been a Halloween candy dispenser. You could turn a dial to send a piece of chocolate, fruit-flavored candy, or gum down a chute.

"It's not that kind of wedding," I explained. "They're just having a small ceremony at city hall."

"That's too bad," said Cassidy. "But that saves money. That's smart." Cassidy paid attention to money in a way that a lot of kids in our class didn't. She knew the prices of things at the grocery store and how much it cost to attend the University of Colorado.

I nodded. That wasn't why they were getting married at city hall, but it was true that they saved money that way. Arne could afford a big wedding, but he just wanted something quiet.

Cassidy didn't notice my silence. "It's okay, you can come over another time. But make it soon, before the basement becomes a mess again," she said cheerfully.

I started to say something about Gwynn's skating lessons but realized I couldn't talk about that either. And I couldn't talk about the purple wall that Arne didn't want. I was starting to feel like an overinflated balloon, getting full of more and more things I couldn't talk about. I just hoped I wouldn't pop.

🌲🌲🌲

At the end of the school day, I rode the chairlift up to Highlands. Mom likes to remind me that kids at most schools can't just walk over to a ski lift, but I tell her that it's one more thing that makes Aspen one of the best places in the world. Cassidy had to go home so they could pick her grandma up from the airport, so I hung out with Jenna and Kelsey, two girls from my class who also like to ski.

When we got to the top at Highlands, I hopped off the ski lift and started to look for a good ski trail down the mountain. Suddenly I heard a voice—a voice that was familiar and unpleasant at the same time. I looked around and saw the boy from the skating rink, the one who had said I had kung flu. His jagged bangs stuck out from under his helmet.

I scooted away. I didn't want to be anywhere near him. Maybe he couldn't tell who I was because I was wearing goggles and a helmet, but maybe he could. I wanted more space between us. Part of me wanted to tell Jenna and Kelsey about him, but maybe they wouldn't understand, just like Arne.

"Go on without me," I told them. "I just want to take a minute and, um, look at the trees."

They shrugged and skied away. "We'll catch you on the next run," called Jenna.

I decided to make a loop into the woods. I pushed on my poles, moving carefully among the trees. While I had made up the excuse about looking at the trees, they really did make me feel calmer. I liked being able to identify them by their bark and branches and needles. It was like seeing friends. The long needles of the ponderosa pine, the squat cones of the piñon pine, the white dots on the needles of the bristlecone pine. As I breathed in their piney scent, my heartbeat slowed down a little.

I heard a noise and a rustle. A black and white dog with thick fur bounded toward me. A woman in an orange and black jacket followed.

"Mojo, come," the woman called. She saw me and smiled. "We're working on search and rescue skills." She bent down to pet Mojo, and I saw SKI PATROL printed on the back of her jacket. Her name tag read Ellen Desilvis.

I let go of my pole and held out my gloved hand. Mojo sniffed it, and I petted him. Now I could see there was a

group of dogs and people doing a training exercise.

"You really shouldn't be skiing alone," said Ellen.

"My friends said they'd catch me on the next run," I said, waving toward the ski lift. "I just wanted a minute by myself."

"Well, do you want to come watch us?" she asked. "Until your friends come back? I'd feel better about you being alone." She said this nicely, not in a bossy way.

"What are you doing?" I asked.

"We help find people who get lost or caught in an avalanche," Ellen explained. "The dogs practice by finding volunteers buried in the snow. Dogs are so much better than people at searching an area in an emergency, when the clock is ticking. What takes us humans three to four hours, Mojo can cover in twenty minutes." At hearing his name, Mojo sat up straighter and looked intently at Ellen.

When Ellen gave the command to search, Mojo started racing across the snow, occasionally pausing before running off again at top speed. Suddenly he stopped and began to dig.

"He's alerting!" said Ellen. "He's telling us he's found a scent." Snow flew everywhere. Ellen knelt down to help, and after a few moments, I could see the orange cap of the person buried in the snow. "Good boy, Mojo!" said Ellen. "Good job!"

The person who came out of the snowbank also

praised Mojo and then started a game of tug-of-war with the dog. Mojo pulled so hard that he looked like he might pitch over backward. Ellen explained that tug-of-war was Mojo's reward for finding the person. Mojo wagged his tail and barked, as if to say, *Let's do it again!*

When I left the rescue team to look for Jenna and Kelsey, I couldn't stop smiling. I loved watching the people and dogs working together, and the dogs acting so excited and proud when they did a good job. Suddenly I knew what special skill I wanted to learn, just like Gwynn and ice skating. I wanted to train a search and rescue dog.

Flurry of Activity

Chapter 6

A dog?" Arne wrinkled his forehead. "Here?" Arne, Mom, and I were waiting for Gwynn's skating lesson to finish. Gwynn looked like she was dancing ballet, gliding smoothly across the ice as she curved her arms in a wide arc.

I turned to Arne. "You said that I should have a project where I get better at something. I want to work with a dog," I announced. "The search and rescue dogs are totally incredible. They work so hard, and they're so enthusiastic about it." I wanted to add that the bond between Ellen and Mojo was something I wanted, too, but because he hadn't been there, I wasn't sure he'd understand. I stuck to the idea of learning a special skill. "The dogs go through a lot of training. They're amazing."

"Well . . . some dogs are amazing," said Arne. "Some dogs are not. When I was a boy, my parents got a dog that we had to give away. He wouldn't stop biting. He bit my sister." Arne scratched his ear. "The dog's name was Astro."

"I do think families today are a lot better about training dogs than when we were kids," said Mom. "We can always hire a trainer if we run into problems."

Arne didn't shake his head or nod. He wobbled his head from side to side. "Mmmmm. That is true."

"So can we go to the shelter?" I asked. I held my breath.

Mom leaned over and whispered in Arne's ear. He nodded. "Maybe, we can sort of go look," he said. "But Corinne, this is a visit just for looking. Not deciding."

"What are we looking at?" asked Gwynn, coming off the ice.

"I want to train a search and rescue dog," I told her. "So I need a dog." Out of the corner of my eye, I saw Arne's shoulders droop.

"Ooh!" said Gwynn. "Yes! A dog! I've always wanted a dog." She took off her headband. Her cheeks were red from working hard. "Alysa Liu has a dog."

"I didn't know you wanted a dog," I said.

"You were supposed to know that through sister brain," said Gwynn, folding her arms.

"Ah," I said. "That explains a lot."

🌲🌲🌲

When we arrived at the animal shelter, I saw some people wearing ski patrol jackets loading bags of food into a van. "Hey!" I said. "That's the same jacket that Ellen wears." It felt like a sign that I was supposed to get a dog!

"Mm-hmm," said Arne. He did not seem very excited to be at the shelter.

I asked the man at the front desk about the ski patrollers outside. "The food for the search and rescue dogs is delivered here," he explained. "We work with them all the time."

"I want a dog I can train to do search and rescue," I explained.

The man, whose name was Kurt, smiled. "Well, let's see who might be a good candidate!"

We followed Kurt through a door to where the dogs were kept. As we walked by each cage, Gwynn let out a long sigh. "Ooh, how about that dog?" she said. A small Chihuahua looked up at us.

"Mmm," said Arne. "I think I would rather a bigger dog." This was a good sign. It meant Arne was actually taking this seriously.

"I think I need a bigger dog to be a rescue dog," I added.

Kurt agreed. "Chihuahuas are really meant to be companions, not working dogs," he explained.

Another kennel had two dogs. "They're a bonded pair," said Kurt. "That means they have a very close relationship and we want them to be adopted together."

"I don't think we're quite ready for that," said Mom.

Corinne

I knew I was lucky to be looking for one dog, so I didn't argue, though the dogs did look very cute curled around each other.

The dog in the next kennel barked furiously at us. "This dog should go to a home with no children," said Kurt. "We're still working on some of his behaviors."

I stood in front of the kennel for a moment, wondering if I could calm the dog down. The card on the cage said his name was Oscar. "It's okay, Oscar," I said soothingly. Oscar stopped barking for about five seconds and then started again.

"Definitely not," said Arne. He barely stopped to look at Oscar. I knew that Arne was right, but the way he said it

made me wince. He didn't even give Oscar a tiny chance. What if Gwynn or I did something that made him feel like just walking away?

I was starting to wonder whether any of the dogs might be right for us, when we stopped at the last cage in the row. The most beautiful dog I'd ever seen looked back at us. I checked the name tag. Her name was Flurry, which made sense because she had a snowy-white nose, feet, and belly, as if she'd just leaped into a pile of snow. Flurry looked like she was smiling at us. As we approached, she stood and walked right up to me.

"We think she was abandoned," said Kurt. "She is definitely used to being with people. She's young. We're guessing around six months."

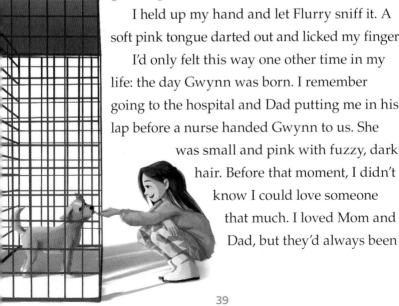

I held up my hand and let Flurry sniff it. A soft pink tongue darted out and licked my finger.

I'd only felt this way one other time in my life: the day Gwynn was born. I remember going to the hospital and Dad putting me in his lap before a nurse handed Gwynn to us. She was small and pink with fuzzy, dark hair. Before that moment, I didn't know I could love someone that much. I loved Mom and Dad, but they'd always been there. Meeting Gwynn was the first time I remembered the moment when love started.

Now, meeting Flurry was the second. I stroked her soft fur through the cage. She stood up on her hind legs and pressed her front paws against the bars between us.

"We have a room where you can get to know each other," said Kurt. "Are you comfortable with dogs?"

"Eh, I don't know," said Arne. He stepped back, away from Flurry and me. "We only meant to come look."

"That's what we said. Just to look. A dog is a big responsibility," said Mom, though she did not sound quite as certain as Arne. "And we're about to have some big changes."

"So what's one more?" I asked. I thought my heart was going to burst. Flurry was meant for us, I just knew it. Mom and Arne had said that we were only coming to look, but I hadn't known that we were going to look at Flurry. I tried to say more but my throat felt too tight.

Arne started toward the exit and took out his phone, ready to move on.

"No!" said Gwynn. "We have to go to the room." She pointed at me. "Cori's heart will be sad, and then mine will be, too. The only thing stronger than sister brain is sister *heart*." She lifted her right foot and set it down next to her left so there was no room in between them. Not quite a stomp, but I knew what it meant. I'd seen it many times in grocery stores and the library. Gwynn wasn't going to move.

Arne turned away from us so we couldn't see his face. I had a teacher who used to do that right before she yelled at us. But Arne didn't yell when he turned back around. His eyes were smiling but his mouth was a wavy line. He looked at Mom. Mom lifted her shoulders slightly and smiled.

"Yes," he said. "Of course. We will go to the room to meet this dog properly."

The room was plain, painted green, with a few toys in it. There were some low benches for us to sit on, and Flurry went from person to person, getting to know us. She picked up a rope toy and brought it to me as if to say, *Play with me!* I tugged on my end and she pulled back, tail wagging. She sat on Mom's foot and leaned back so Mom could scratch behind her ears. She thumped her foot when Gwynn rubbed her tummy, and then she brought a ball to Gwynn.

She went to Arne last. I held my breath.

Flurry stood in front of Arne and looked at him. "Hey, hey," said Arne softly. They both looked like they were trying to make up their minds about each other.

Flurry sat down right in front of Arne. Then she stuck out her paw, like a person offering to shake hands. A smile broke out over Arne's face.

"Oh my," said Arne. "Such nice manners!" He took

Flurry's paw and bobbed it up and down a few times. Then he petted her awkwardly on the head. Gwynn and I exchanged a glance, not daring to say a word. What would happen next?

Arne looked at Mom, and Mom smiled. "I guess the dog is a wedding present?" said Arne.

Gwynn raised her arms up in the air. "Yes!" Gwynn and I grabbed each other and started jumping up and down. Then Flurry joined us, barking. I think she knew she had a new home!

That night, Flurry curled up in a circle between our beds after sniffing the entire room, and Gwynn and I watched her sleep. I couldn't believe she was ours. Maybe if Gwynn hadn't said anything, we wouldn't have made it to the green room. Maybe if Flurry hadn't offered her paw, we'd be home without her. But everything had happened just right. Flurry was a member of our family.

Arne hadn't wanted to get her right away, but he seemed okay now. He even smiled when we stopped at the pet store to get a bed, a collar, and some food. Part of me couldn't help wondering, though, what would happen if things didn't go right, if Flurry did something wrong. Would Arne change his mind again?

Day to Remember
Chapter 7

*B*efore long, we couldn't imagine life without Flurry. We learned her habits, like her way of turning in a circle before lying down or telling us the water bowl was empty by banging on it until it flipped over. I'd pat the spot next to me and say, "Load up," the way I'd heard the ski patrollers call to the dogs to get on the ski lift, and Flurry would jump up for a snuggle.

Coming home from school was way better when Flurry was there to greet us. She made Gwynn and me feel like the most important people in the world. We developed a routine: we would have a snack and then play for a bit before we did our homework. Flurry's favorite game was hide-and-seek. One of us would hold Flurry, and then the other one would hide and call her from the hiding place. Our apartment was not very big, so it usually didn't take long. When Gwynn hid, it was even better because she could fit in smaller spaces, like in a kitchen cabinet or under the couch.

When Flurry found one of us, you could tell that she

was really proud of herself. She'd bounce around in a circle and bark, as if to say, *I did it!* Then we would reward her with tug-of-war and tell her she was the best, smartest dog in the world.

One time, Gwynn held on to Flurry and I pretended to run into the kitchen, but then I turned and moved stealthily back down the hall to hide in the bathroom. I slid behind the door and waited, perfectly still, before calling Flurry. Then I noticed that the shower curtain was moving. Just a little bit, but it was definitely moving. What could be in the shower? Or, *who* could be in the shower? I screamed. Which made Gwynn scream in the hallway.

Flurry burst out of the shower and began licking me. I collapsed on the floor, laughing.

"You scared me," said Gwynn.

"You were supposed to hold on to Flurry!" I said. "I wasn't done hiding."

"That's not what she told me," said Gwynn. "She told me that I should let her go."

"I guess you wanted a turn at hiding, huh, girl?" I asked, rubbing Flurry's neck. "We must think alike, both hiding in the bathroom." Flurry's eyes twinkled.

"Flurry must have sister brain, too," declared Gwynn.

🌲🌲🌲

Day to Remember

Gwynn and I wanted to bring Flurry to city hall for the wedding, but Mom had arranged for her to go to the vet and spend the night. Mom wore a dark red dress that made her look like a movie star. Arne wore his favorite gray suit with a flower in the lapel. When they looked at each other, they looked very, very happy.

I thought I would feel different after they got married, but I felt mostly the same. Mom was still Mom, and Arne was still Arne, but now they wore shiny gold wedding rings.

After the ceremony, Arne had presents for Gwynn and me. He knelt down and handed us each a black velvet box. Each box contained a necklace with three flat gold heart charms. The biggest charm on mine had my name on it, and the biggest charm on Gwynn's had her name on it.

"I have married your mother," Arne told us. "And I won't try to replace your father. But I want to remember the day that we officially became a family. I love you all, and I will do my best by you."

"This is the most beautiful necklace in the world," said Gwynn. She tilted her head forward so Mom could fasten it for her. I could put my necklace on by myself. I patted the charms, making sure the heart with my name on it faced out.

"What are the other two hearts for?" asked Gwynn.

"Hmm . . . ," said Arne. "What do you think?"

"One for you, and one for Mommy?" asked Gwynn.

"That would leave out Corinne," said Arne.

"And Flurry," I said, wanting to be fair.

"I don't want to leave anyone out," protested Gwynn. She tucked her chin down, trying to look at the necklace while she was wearing it. Then she whispered to me, "I don't want Daddy to be left out either."

"How about this," I said. "One heart is for all the people we've loved but are no longer here with us. Like Ye-ye." Ye-ye was my dad's father, who had died before we were born. "One heart is for all the people we love who are with us now. One heart is for all the people we don't know yet but will love in the future. Past, present, future."

"Oh," Gwynn said, nodding. "I like that. A few weeks ago, Flurry would have been a future love, but now she's a present love."

"That is very beautiful, girls," said Arne.

A Special Night
Chapter 8

*A*fter the ceremony, we went to dinner with some of Mom's and Arne's friends at a restaurant called Peak. Mom was friends with the owner, and he gave us a table in the back. Everyone kept asking us what we thought of the ceremony, and I didn't know what to say.

"It's the only wedding I've ever been to," I said.

Gwynn said, "This was my favorite part," and showed off her necklace as her answer, but we didn't get the necklaces until after the ceremony, so I wasn't sure that counted.

Mostly, I tried to stay on my best behavior and not make a hole in my tights or lose a shoe. The wedding cake had coconut, which I am not crazy about, so I only had a small bite.

When Dad came to get us, it was a relief to take a break from talking about the wedding. He texted us when he was outside the restaurant. Gwynn and I gave Mom and Arne hugs and kisses, and then we quickly changed into our regular clothes in the restaurant's fancy bathroom.

Corinne

"How was it?" asked Dad as we climbed into his car. I studied his face to see if he was upset, but it seemed like he could have been asking about anything, like a movie or a spelling test.

"It was magical," said Gwynn. She put her hand on her necklace and opened her mouth to say something, but I grabbed her arm and shook my head. I didn't think Dad would want to know about the necklaces, even if one of the hearts represented him.

I thought of something to say. "The wedding part was over pretty quickly," I said. "I thought getting married would take more time." Suddenly I realized that Dad was not driving us to his house. "Where are we going?" I asked.

"Well," said Dad, "I thought I would do something special with you girls, too." Dad winked at me as he turned off the main road, and I saw where we were headed— Buttermilk! This time Dad took us to the area where they sold food, to a round table that had a fire pit in the middle of it. The fire danced and glowed.

"Daddy," said Gwynn. "That table is reserved." She pointed to a sign on the table.

Dad smiled. "That's right. It's reserved for us!"

We sat on the bench that curved around the table, and a woman came over to take our order. "We'll get the s'mores and three hot chocolates," said Dad, flashing his ski badge.

A Special Night

"And I'm an employee here."

"Oh," said the woman. "I'm not sure the discount applies here." Dad frowned. "But I'll go check," she added.

The woman brought over mugs of hot chocolate and a plate with marshmallows, graham crackers, and chocolate bars. She handed each of us a long stick for toasting the marshmallows.

"I got you the discount, Mr. Tan," she said to Dad with a wink. "But don't tell my boss!"

"Thanks," said Dad.

It was special to be ordering dessert at our own private fire pit. Usually we brought our own meals, or maybe stood in line and ordered food on special occasions. I thought of the credit card that Arne had put on my ski pass. I could probably pay for the cocoa and s'mores and Arne wouldn't mind, but I knew Dad wouldn't like that.

I slid the toasted marshmallow off the stick and onto a graham cracker and then put a square of chocolate and another graham cracker on top. The heat of the marshmallow melted the chocolate a little, and when I took a bite, the marshmallow squished out the sides. *Delicious.*

"This is much better than cake with coconut," said Gwynn, taking an oozy bite of s'more. "Coconut tastes like wood shavings."

"And how do you know what wood shavings taste like?" asked Dad. "Have you eaten them, like a beaver?" He and Gwynn giggled and sipped hot cocoa.

Our breath made little cloud puffs in the cold dark. The fire felt warm and good. The red and gold flames flickered and snapped in the darkness. "This is the best part of the day," I said. I put another marshmallow at the end of the stick and held it over the fire. The marshmallow turned golden brown.

"The fire is making my necklace hot!" exclaimed Gwynn. She was sitting closer to the fire than I was.

"What necklace is that?" asked Dad.

"Oh." Gwynn looked at me guiltily. "Arne gave us necklaces after the wedding."

I didn't know what to say, so I said, "Sorry." And then

A Special Night

I pulled my jacket closed to cover my own necklace.

"Corinne, it's fine," said Dad. "Now Arne is an important part of your life. But I have a gift, too!" He opened his phone and showed us. "One of my buddies got Eileen Gu to sign a poster. I didn't bring it because I didn't want it to get crumpled, but this is what it looks like." The poster showed Eileen coming off the lip of the half-pipe, mid-twist. I could make out her signature at the bottom.

"Wow! Autographed and everything!" said Gwynn. "Thank you, Daddy."

"You didn't have to get us a gift," I said.

"I thought you liked Eileen Gu," he said.

"We do! We do!" I didn't want Dad to feel like he had to compete with this day, or with Arne. But trying to explain that might make him feel worse. "I . . . I love this." I took a deep breath, taking in the cold night air. "And I love this, too," I gestured to the faint outline of the mountains against the dark sky. "Everything is better outside."

"That's how I feel, too," said Dad. He took a sip of his hot chocolate and sighed. "The cold mountain air clears the mind. You always loved being on the mountain, even when you were really little."

"I remember wearing that harness to ski with you when I was little," I said.

"Oh yes!" said Dad. "You skied in front, and I would

hold the leashes for the harness. If I wanted you to turn, I'd pull gently on the leash."

"I don't have memories like that," complained Gwynn. "All I remember is falling down a lot."

I was lucky to have happy memories of skiing with Mom and Dad when I was little—before they stopped getting along. Gwynn and I would just have to make our own happy memories now—some with Mom and Arne, some with Dad, and, of course, some with Flurry.

Flurry, Search!

Chapter 9

We spent the night and most of the next day at Dad's, and then he dropped us off late in the afternoon at Arne's house. Flurry greeted us at the door, so we gave her hugs first. Mom came to the door and waved to Dad.

"Did you have a good time with Dad?" asked Mom.

"We did! We had s'mores at Buttermilk at this place with our own fire pit and everything," said Gwynn.

"Sounds pretty fancy," said Mom.

I gave Mom a hug. "Did you guys have fun going away?"

"Actually," said Mom, "we stayed here. To help with a secret project."

"You're going to give it away!" said Arne, joining us. "I didn't know I had married someone so indiscreet." He gave Mom a kiss on the cheek with a big smacking noise.

"What is it?" asked Gwynn. She paused, thinking. "*Another* dog?"

"Oh good heavens, no," said Arne. "One is enough."

It wasn't fair of Arne to act like Flurry was such a

handful. She was standing calmly in the foyer, like the rest of us.

"Come upstairs," said Mom. We followed Mom and Arne up the stairs.

The door to our bedroom was closed. "Are you girls ready to move in?" Arne asked. He put his hand on the doorknob. Flurry sat down and stared at the closed door.

Gwynn and I looked at each other, excited and curious. What was Arne up to? Then Arne flung the door open. "Ta-da!" he cried.

The old, grown-up guest room was gone. In its place was a beautiful new bedroom for me and Gwynn!

"Holy cow!" said Gwynn. "Are we on television? This looks like something on TV!"

"I talked to my decorator about the purple wall," said Arne. "And she said, why just a wall?"

I looked at the wall. It did have purple in it, but there was more than that. It was a whole mural of mountains and trees. "It's like a mountain inside our bedroom!" I said, touching the wall with my hand. "I love it."

"That's what the designer was going for," said Arne. "Think of this as your own ski chalet."

The bunk bed wasn't just any old bunk bed. The upper bed had a railing shaped like a mountain range and was covered in cozy pillows and blankets. The bottom was just

as snug. Each bed was its own little comfy nest. Flurry
leaped onto the bottom bunk and sniffed around. I imag-
ined snuggling in my pj's with Flurry and watching the
snow fall outside the window.

At the other end of the room was a fireplace. "We could
make s'mores in our room!" said Gwynn.

"We'll have some rules about food in the room," said
Mom. "But yes, we will definitely have s'mores in here
one day."

Gwynn threw her arms up in the air. "Arne is magical!"
she squealed.

Arne laughed. "Arne has a wonderful interior designer,"
he said. "I am glad you girls are happy."

Happy didn't seem like a big enough word to describe
Gwynn's excitement. She kept running around the room
touching everything. She wanted the top bunk, then the
bottom bunk, then said I could decide because both were
so great.

I was excited, too, but I also had questions. "So, where
would be a good place to hang up a poster?" I asked, thinking about the Eileen Gu poster Dad had gotten us.

Mom hesitated. "You can hang it in the closet." We had
a walk-in closet for all our clothes.

"Um, okay," I said. I felt bad that the poster Dad gave us
would end up in the closet, but the room was so pretty just

the way it was. I wished I could have an uncomplicated kind of happy, like Gwynn, with this beautiful new bedroom.

🌲🌲🌲

I couldn't tell Cassidy about the new bedroom, because then she'd want to see it. And then she'd *know* know about Arne. I didn't want to tell her about Gwynn's skating competition yet, because Cassidy thought competitive skaters were snobs. I was even afraid to go over to Cassidy's house, because then she'd want to come over to mine. So when my Dad said he had a friend who could meet us at the park to work with Flurry, I jumped at the chance to do something with Cassidy.

It was Dad's and Cassidy's first time meeting Flurry. "I wish I had a dog," said Cassidy. "But Jake is allergic." Jake was Cassidy's little brother. Then she handed me a bag. "I made Flurry a jacket."

The jacket was made of purple fleece, with a hole for Flurry's head and a buckle for under her tummy. "It's so cool!" I said. "Thanks!" Cassidy had even stitched Flurry's name in cursive in blue thread across one side. She really could make anything. Flurry smiled and wagged her tail. I think she liked the jacket.

Dad knelt down to pet her. "Hi, Flurry," he said. Flurry looked at Dad and then offered her paw, just like she had done with Arne. Dad laughed and then introduced us to his friend Zach, who worked with search and rescue dogs at Buttermilk.

"Did you train her to shake hands?" Zach asked.

I shook my head. "Nope, it's just something she does."

"I like that. It shows intelligence and awareness. She focuses on people. All good traits," Zach told me. "What else can she do?"

I showed Zach how I played hide-and-seek with Flurry. Cassidy held on to her while I ran away and hid behind a stand of trees, holding a blue-and-orange braided rope, one of Flurry's favorite toys.

"Come find me!" I called. Peeking through the branches, I could see Flurry put her nose down to the ground and make her way toward me. "Good girl!" I said, when she found me. Zach was pleased.

"Now you can build on that skill," said Zach. "Here, let's dig a couple of holes in the snow, and I'll show you how we train our dogs." He handed us each a small folding shovel.

"Does it matter that Flurry will see our hiding places?" I asked as we dug.

"No, it's fine. She's using her eyes, but she'll start using her nose, too. Dogs have three hundred million olfactory receptors for smelling, compared with six million in people.

She also has a bigger part of her brain devoted to smelling," said Zach.

Cassidy offered to hide in one of the snow holes. She crawled in, and I gave her the rope toy to keep with her. Then Dad and I covered the hole up with snow.

Zach turned to Flurry. "Flurry, search!"

Flurry started to get excited, barking and tugging on the leash. I'd never used the word *search* before, but Flurry seemed to know what it meant. As soon as Zach let go of the leash, Flurry put her nose to the ground and sniffed her way to the hole where Cassidy was buried.

"Now, learn to look for signs that she's alerting, or telling you that she's found something," said Zach. "My dog barks and her tail wags so fast that it almost vibrates." Ellen had used the word *alerting,* too, with Mojo.

Flurry pushed her two front paws into the snow, right on top of where Cassidy was. She had an intense, serious look on her face. I wondered if that was her alerting face.

"Cassidy, let Flurry know she did a great job. Heap on the praise!" said Zach.

Cassidy crawled from the hole and jumped up and down. "You saved me! You saved me!" she told Flurry.

"Now play tug-of-war with her. That's her big reward. We like doing that rather than using treats." Cassidy swung the rope in the air, and Flurry jumped and caught it and began to pull. She was really excited!

"I want to go next!" I said.

"Corinne, you take the rope toy and go hide in a different hole," Zach said. "And let's see how she listens to you," he said to Dad.

I took the rope toy and ran to one of the other holes. Cassidy helped cover me up. I listened really carefully. Sounds were muffled, but I was pretty sure I heard Dad say, "Search!"

For a few moments, nothing happened. Then suddenly, a bit of light filtered in. Flurry had broken into the snowbank! I jumped up and praised her. "You did it, Flurry! Good girl!" I offered her the rope toy, and Flurry grabbed it and pulled.

"She's so determined!" said Dad.

"We look for dogs with a lot of drive," said Zach. "Flurry looks to be a high-drive dog. I bet she can keep going for a while."

We played a few more times, with Dad, Cassidy, and I taking turns hiding in the snow. I worked on getting Flurry hyped up before the search. "Can you find Dad, Flurry? Can you find him? Where is he? Search!" It was like winding up a toy before letting it go and then watching it spring into action. Flurry was excited every single time.

Zach told us that when Flurry got good at finding

people using scent, we could do things to make it harder, like having different people walk around to add smells or burying clothes in the snow. "Get an old sweater or something," he said. "Have someone wear it for a few days to scent it. Then go bury it in the snow."

"I can have my brother do that," said Cassidy. "Jake's plenty stinky."

I loved having a plan for training Flurry to be a search and rescue dog. Then I thought of something else. "Should she have a vest?" I asked.

"Our dogs know that when the vest goes on, it's time to work," said Zach. "We call it 'going up the hill.' You can get a vest so she knows you mean business. Vests also have handles, so you can lift up your dog or give her a hand if you need to."

"The jacket I made can be for casual wear, and the vest can be for work," said Cassidy. Flurry barked as if to say, *Yes! Get me a vest!* We laughed.

Zach told us about his dog. She was trained to jump on his back so he could ski with her where they needed to go. "We want the dogs to save their energy for the search, not get tired out from getting there or get hurt from working too hard."

I added that to my mental list of things to teach Flurry.

"Now," said Zach to Cassidy and me, "I have a question

for you two. What should you do if you get lost in the mountains?"

I couldn't imagine getting lost in the mountains. I knew them so well. But I figured it would be rude not to answer Zach's question. "Go look for an adult?" I asked.

"Make a flag out of your coat?" asked Cassidy, which was a very Cassidy-like answer.

"I can see why you'd say that," said Zach. "But think of it like this. If you're moving around, looking for an adult, and the adult is moving around, looking for you, then you have two moving objects trying to find each other. It's much better for you to stay put. And while I like your creativity," he said to Cassidy, "one of our biggest concerns in the rescue business is people getting hypothermia—or losing too much body heat. So keep your coat on. Stay dry and warm. Instead of making a flag, keep calling for help. It wouldn't hurt to keep a whistle attached to your coat."

"People should just be more careful," said Cassidy.

"No one ever intends to get lost," said Zach. "Weather turns sour, parents lose track of a kid, someone gets turned around on a trail. It happens all the time. We train our dogs to have good skills, but people need them, too."

Flurry came over and lay down at my feet. She looked at me intently. "You two have a really good bond," said Zach. "That might be the most important thing of all."

Zongzi Time
Chapter 10

*A*fter meeting Flurry for the first time, Cassidy kept asking to see her again. I kept making up dentist appointments as excuses, but I knew I was getting into trouble when Cassidy grumbled, "What kind of dentist do you have? Does she work on one tooth at a time?" Cassidy also started noticing little things, like my new phone. "Why did you get a new one?" she asked. "Did the old one break?"

"No, my mom wanted Gwynn to have it," I said, which was technically true. Arne had bought me a new phone so I could take sharper photos of Flurry, and Mom gave my old phone to Gwynn in case she ever needed to make a call.

I promised myself that I would tell Cassidy the whole truth eventually, but for now, I just needed a little more time to get used to the changes myself.

So much was going on. Gwynn's training for her first competition was getting really intense. And I wanted to get used to the new house before bringing Cassidy over. Arne had more rules than we had at our old house, like rinsing the dishes before putting them in the dishwasher and keeping our shoes in the garage instead of by the front door. They were little things, but they added up, like trying to pat your head while rubbing your tummy while hopping on one foot.

Finally, I got the idea that Cassidy could come over to my mom's new restaurant. Mom had named it Kuai Le, which has two meanings. Depending on how you said it, it could mean happiness, as in *xin nian kuai le,* or "happy new year"—or it could mean "soon." I figured it meant that anyone buying Mom's food would be happy very soon!

The restaurant would open in two weeks. Mom was still working out some details on the menu and waiting for approval from the city.

Cassidy and I walked in. The restaurant was bright and white, with a couple of lime green tables and chairs. The menu behind the counter showed pictures of what people could order—savory pancakes called *cong you bing,* dumplings called *jiaozi,* and bubble tea.

Cassidy's mouth fell open. "It's so pretty! And it smells so good!"

"You get to come to the back," I told her. "Only special people—like us!—get to go behind the counter." We went into the kitchen, which was small but very clean and efficient. Mom was making one of my favorites, *zongzi.*

Corinne

Zongzi is rice and other goodies wrapped tightly inside bamboo leaves and tied with string.

Mom greeted us with a smile and showed us how she wrapped the zongzi. She overlapped two long bamboo leaves and created a bowl shape in the center by turning the ends of the leaves up. She spooned in rice, added pork and mushrooms—my favorite kind of filling—and put more rice on top. Then she wrapped the leaves down around the rice until it was shaped almost like a wedge of cheese.

"It's really tricky," Mom said. "My mother taught me to cut the strings ahead of time so you can tie them up more easily. But it's still a lot of work. Maybe it's too much to put on the menu."

"You have to sell zongzi!" I said. "It's the perfect food for skiing. The rice stays warm for a long time, so you can keep it in your pocket. And once you eat it, you have energy to ski for a long time!"

Mom's phone rang. "I have to take this," she said. "It's about Gwynn's—"

I coughed really loud. I was afraid Mom would say *costume,* and then Cassidy would find out that Gwynn had started ice skating competitively. Cassidy gave me a puzzled look. "Gwynn is having some problems in school," I whispered.

Cassidy looked around the kitchen. It was just the two

of us now. "Let's try to make a zongzi while your mom is on the phone!" she said. Cassidy couldn't resist making new things.

"I've never made one," I said. "But I'm really good at eating them."

Cassidy laughed. "C'mon," she said. She washed her hands in the big sink and then took out two long bamboo leaves from a bowl of water, just as Mom had done it. She made sure to put the shiny side of the leaves facing out and then neatly flipped them to make the bowl. "How much rice should we put in?"

"Maybe one big spoonful?" I suggested.

Cassidy held the bamboo leaves while I added the rice. Then I put in some pork chunks and mushrooms and added more rice on top. When I was done, Cassidy tried turning and folding the leaves. "Is this right?" she asked.

The shape of the zongzi Mom made was triangular. Ours looked more like a brick. "Squeeze that end a little," I said. Mom had precut lengths of string and left them on the table. I picked up one. "Maybe the shape will get better when we tie it," I said.

Cassidy was quiet for a minute as I looped the string around the zongzi. I knew I was supposed to tie it in a way that would keep the leaves from unfolding. Cassidy stared at the zongzi, as if trying to figure out the shape. Finally, she said, "Cori."

"Yes?" I didn't know what kind of knot Mom used, so I was making one up.

"I think you tied the zongzi to my thumb!" Cassidy held up her hand, and sure enough, the zongzi dangled from it.

"Oh no!" I got a pair of scissors and carefully cut the string. "Thumbs are not part of zongzi!" I laughed.

We tried again, and by the time Mom finished her phone call, we had made a pretty decent one.

"Look at what you girls did!" said Mom. "I might have to hire you to help me back here." She inspected the zongzi. "Not bad for a first try," she said. "Let me show you a few more tricks."

We spent all afternoon in the kitchen helping Mom make zongzi and tasting other items for the menu. Mom even had a little television we could watch. "Hey, there's ice skating," Mom said, flipping through the channels.

Cassidy craned her neck to see who was skating. "Oh, that girl from France. She's pretty good."

I was surprised. "I thought you didn't like ice skating."

"I don't like the girls around *here* who ice skate," said

Cassidy, correcting me. "They all think they're so great."

Mom looked at me. I lowered my head, pretending to be intensely interested in chopping green onions. "It takes a lot of hard work and confidence to become a great skater. They all have to start somewhere," Mom said lightly.

"That's true," admitted Cassidy. "But there's this one girl at school, Emmeline Daniels. I bumped into her at the rink once while she was skating backward and she made a huge deal out of it. Like I had done it on purpose."

I had been there. Emmeline had gone flying backward over Cassidy's skate and landed with a huge thump on her behind. Emmeline practically told the whole rink that Cassidy was a klutz.

"Hmm," said Mom. "That's unfortunate. But maybe other girls aren't like Emmeline." I bit my lip and hoped she wouldn't say anything else.

"Anyone home?" a voice called from the front.

Dad! He was picking me up for the night. I ran and gave him a hug. He smelled like sweat and ski wax. Dad and I walked back to the kitchen.

"Hmm . . . Gwynn, you look different!" Dad said playfully to Cassidy. Cassidy squatted down and pretended to be Gwynn, which was pretty funny because Cassidy is taller than I am.

"I was hoping you could drop Cassidy off at home, after

you pick up Gwynn at Pippa's house," said Mom. Pippa was Gwynn's best friend.

"Or you could drop Cassidy off first, and then pick up Gwynn," I said, hoping Dad would get the hint. I didn't want Gwynn and Cassidy to overlap, in case Gwynn talked about skating.

"I thought Gwynn was going to be here," said Dad. "Otherwise, I would have picked her up on the way over here." His voice got a tiny bit tense.

"It's not that far," said Mom. "Pippa and Cassidy live very close to each other."

"That's not the point," said Dad. "I would like to make that decision." He emphasized the word *I*. Mom looked up at the ceiling and blew a strand of hair out of her eyes, which was a sign that she was also getting mad.

"Let's wash our hands and go try out the chairs in the front," said Cassidy quickly. "I want to see what they feel like."

I followed her numbly. I hated it when my parents fought, even a little bit, even though they were divorced. I felt like I had swallowed a wheelbarrow full of rocks.

Cassidy grabbed my arm once we had sat down. "It stinks, doesn't it?" she whispered. Cassidy didn't really want to try out the chairs. She wanted to get me away from my parents. Cassidy's parents were also divorced, though they'd split up when she was little. My parents had been divorced officially for two years. Mom said the stress from the pandemic had done in their marriage.

I wiped my eyes. "Yeah," I said. "They have a way of talking to each other that just makes me feel terrible. They don't do it all the time, but when they do, it makes me so sad."

Cassidy got up and put her arm around me. "I know that feeling," she said. At that moment, I wanted to tell Cassidy the truth about everything, but I couldn't. If I lost her as a friend, I didn't know what I would do.

Wishes on Stars

Chapter 11

By the time we got to Dad's house, the sky was dark, but Dad was in a good mood again. He started cooking chicken and vegetables for stir-fry, and Gwynn was admiring Dad's skiing trophies on the top shelf of the bookcase. She loves looking at them.

"I want to win a trophy," said Gwynn with a sigh.

"Maybe you'll get one for ice skating," I said.

Gwynn nodded and showed us her routine. She hummed the song under her breath while she skated across the bare floor in her socks. "This is what I'm working on. It's called a waltz jump."

She leaped into the air, spun, and landed on one foot, with the other foot sticking out, like an arabesque. Her face lit up when she stuck the landing. "Now I just need to do that on the ice."

"That looks good," said Dad, watching from the kitchen. "Don't wave your arms around though, Gwynn. You'll throw yourself off balance."

Wishes on Stars

"That's what Ms. Margot says!" said Gwynn. "No windmill arms."

From the kitchen we heard the pop of the rice cooker. "You can skate to the table," said Dad. "Dinner's ready!"

After dinner, Dad told us to put on our coats and hats and mittens. Then he dragged our futon mattress to the back deck.

"Are we sleeping out here?" I asked.

"Nope," said Dad. He went back inside and brought out blankets. Then we lay down on the futon, snuggling together. He pointed up to the sky. "There's a meteor shower tonight!" Dad explained that meteors could be seen any night, but once in a while, you could see a bunch of them in a short period of time. That was a meteor shower.

We had to let our eyes adapt to the dark to really see the stars. There were so many! And then every minute or so, a pinprick of light would fly across the sky.

"I think we should make a wish every time we see a shooting star," said Gwynn.

"They're not really stars," I corrected her. In school, my teacher had explained this during science. "They're actually very hot rocks."

"Well, you can make your wishes on rocks," said Gwynn. "I'll make *my* wishes on stars."

I didn't tell Gwynn that stars were big balls of gas. We

started making lots of wishes. Gwynn wished for gummy bears and a trophy at the ice skating competition. Dad wished for customers who tipped well, good knees, and children who did not snore. Gwynn and I laughed when he said that.

"We do not snore!" I said. "*You* snore!" Sometimes Dad snored so loudly that we could hear him through the wall.

"I do not snore!" Dad protested. "I sleep like a little kitten." That made us laugh even harder.

I wished that Flurry and I would make a good rescue team and for a good grade on my long-division test. I also wished that I could meet Eileen Gu. Then I made a private wish: I wished that Cassidy already knew all my secrets—and that she would stay my friend no matter what.

Dad pointed to a cluster of stars. "Those are the Pleiades. People call them the Seven Sisters."

"What are their names?" asked Gwynn.

"I think one of them is Maia. I don't remember the others. They're all Greek names. But the first people to write about the Pleiades were the Chinese." Dad straightened up a little. You could tell he was proud about that.

"Ooh," said Gwynn, snuggling deeper into the blankets.

"Maybe one is Gwynn and one is Cori," I said. "And they travel across the sky together."

"Maybe one of the stars accidentally forgets the book she's supposed to read for school," said Gwynn.

Corinne

For a second I thought Gwynn was adding on to my story, but then I realized she was talking about herself. "Oh no, did you really?" I asked. We try to keep a set of clothes at each house, but schoolwork is something we're supposed to take with us back and forth. I'm always afraid I'm going to forget an important piece of paper for school.

Gwynn tucked her chin down. "Yes." Another star flew by. "I wish I hadn't forgotten my book," Gwynn said.

"We can check the library tomorrow," Dad said. "And I have neighbors with a son your age—I can ask if they have a copy. We'll find a way."

Gwynn perked up. "Really?"

"Really," said Dad. "Don't worry. Everybody makes mistakes. We just have to figure out how to solve them."

Sister Power

Chapter 12

Mom had an idea for getting the word out about Kuai Le. She made tons of small zongzi and added tags with the restaurant's address and website. Then she put them in an insulated backpack and walked us over to the gondola, which would take us to Ajax. (That's everyone's nickname for Aspen Mountain.) Gwynn and I would pass the zongzi out to skiers and tell them about the restaurant.

"Be sure to smile," Mom said. "And pronounce the name carefully, so people will remember it, okay?" She demonstrated, saying *kuai le* slowly. *Kuai* sounded like the first syllable in "quiet," and *le* sounded like the beginning of "luck." "Come back to the restaurant when you're done."

"What about Flurry?" I asked. "Flurry is used to us coming home after school."

"I'll go get her," said Mom. "So she's not lonely."

While the gondola took us up the mountain, I started to worry. What if nobody wanted a zongzi? What if they said it would give them coronavirus? What would I even say? I wanted the restaurant to do well, though. It was Mom's dream.

When we got off the gondola and put on our skis, clusters of people were standing around the station.

"Should we talk to some of these people?" asked Gwynn.

I hesitated. "Um, if they're hanging out here, they're probably planning to eat at Sundeck, so let's not bother them." Sundeck was the restaurant at the top of the mountain. "Let's go down a ways first."

Gwynn and I took the Copper trail, which would go through Silver Dip and Deer Park and then feed into Spar Gulch. Spar Gulch is a valley between two big ridges that could take us back to town.

"What a beautiful day!" said Gwynn. She was right. The sky was perfectly blue with just a few clouds, and it wasn't too windy. "Perfect for skiing!"

But maybe not for passing out zongzi, I thought, as Gwynn spotted a group of skiers off to the side of the trail and headed toward them. "They look like they're busy," I said to Gwynn, making another excuse not to talk to anyone.

"No one's too busy for zongzi!" said Gwynn confidently. She skied right up to the group of people. "Would any of you like to try a zongzi from my mom's restaurant, Kuai Le? It's going to be opening downtown next week." Her voice was bright and friendly.

One of the women pushed up her goggles. "Of course! Is it Chinese food?" She looked really excited, which made me feel good.

Gwynn nodded and motioned for me to come over. I turned around so Gwynn could reach in my backpack and get the zongzi out with a pair of tongs that Mom had put in there. A few of the other women held out their hands—they were also interested!

"Look at that," said the first woman. She was admiring the wrapping. "It's all so environmental, using leaves."

"They smell delicious," said her friend. "I've been working up an appetite!"

"That smells meaty. Do you have anything vegetarian?" asked another woman.

"The ones with red strings have mushrooms and peanuts," I reminded Gwynn. She nodded and handed over a zongzi with red string. The woman smiled and said thanks.

Now people were crowding around to see what was happening. Gloved hands seemed to appear everywhere. "You can get zongzi, dumplings, and other treats at the newest restaurant in Aspen," said Gwynn loudly, "Kuai Le."

I took off the backpack so I could help hand out the zongzi. "Come to Kuai Le!" I said. "The address is on the tag." Within about ten minutes, all the samples were gone. The skiers were hungry!

"You were incredible," I told Gwynn. "I don't think I could talk to a bunch of strangers that way."

"I felt braver because you were here," admitted Gwynn. "Also, I really thought people would want to taste the zongzi!"

"They sure did!" I said. We could take our time going down the mountain now. We made long lines back and forth down the slope. I had thought it would take longer to give out the zongzi, and now we had time to play. I saw a little grove of trees and got an idea.

"This would be a great place for a shrine!" I said, remembering the Calvin and Hobbes shrine we'd seen with Dad. As someone who loved Aspen and the mountains, I wanted to have a shrine, too.

"It would," agreed Gwynn. "What kind of shrine should it be?" This was an important question.

I thought about how Gwynn was able to do something that I thought I couldn't do, give out the zongzi, but only because I was there. We were an unbreakable team. "How about a sister shrine?"

"I love it!" cried Gwynn.

We skied over to the grove. The trees formed a horse-shoe, an excellent sheltered place to put something special. One of the trees had a low, broad branch that was protected by a thick roof of branches. "This is perfect!"

"What can we add?" pondered Gwynn. "We both wear

scrunchies," she said, removing the scrunchie from her hair and looping it over one of the smaller branches.

"That's good," I said. I looked in the backpack. There was an extra tag on a piece of string from the zongzi. "How about this tag, because it's something we did together?"

"Yes," said Gwynn. "I wish we had something purple, for our bedroom."

"We can always come back," I said. "We can add to it." I hunted around on the ground and picked up seven small pinecones. I arranged them on the branch. "These are for the Pleiades, the sister stars."

"This bigger one is you, *jie jie*," said Gwynn. "And this smaller one is me."

"*Mei mei*," I said. Little sister.

"Now something for wishes," said Gwynn. She pulled a small piece of fabric from her pocket. "I was saving this to show Pippa what my skating costume looks like, but I'll leave it here. It's for my wish to win a trophy at the skating competition."

"I want Flurry to be a good rescue dog," I said. I picked up a pinecone and stuck four twigs in it so it looked kind of like a dog. "This will do for now."

"It still doesn't feel special enough," said Gwynn. She stood back and stared at the branch. Then she reached her hands behind her neck. "Help me take off my necklace."

"The necklace Arne gave us?" Gwynn wore her necklace all the time. "But what if someone comes along and takes it?"

"No one knows this shrine is here," said Gwynn confidently. "Besides, they'd only want it if they were also named Gwynn." When I hesitated, she added, "It's only until we can add some other things. This is just to keep the shrine special until we can come back."

"Okay." We would come back soon. I pulled off my gloves so I could release the delicate clasp. Gwynn carefully laid the necklace over the branch so we could see the three hearts shining against the dark wood. Past, present, and future loves. I hugged her. "I've loved you your whole life."

Gwynn hugged me back. "And I've loved you *my* whole life," she said. She put her hand in mine. "Now we have a shrine, just for us," she said. Snow was starting to fall, leaving tiny snowflakes on the log. It was so peaceful, standing among the trees with Gwynn.

"We will always belong here," I told Gwynn. "No matter what happens." Having a place that was just ours made me feel better. It wasn't Dad's place or Arne's place. It was our space, our home, where we made the rules.

"Promise we'll come back soon," said Gwynn.

I looked around, memorizing the spot on the mountain. "We will," I said. "And we'll bring more things for the shrine." I was already thinking of what we could add: a photograph, something purple from our room, and maybe one of Flurry's toys.

Gwynn and I skied the rest of the way down the hill. We glided at the exact same speed, switching places as we zigzagged our way to the bottom. After such a perfect afternoon, it felt as though we could do anything as long as we were together.

Overheard

Chapter 13

*A*fter we reached the bottom of Ajax, we took off our skis and walked back to Kuai Le. Flurry was outside the restaurant with a bowl of water, her leash wrapped around a tree. She wagged her tail furiously when she saw us, and we stopped to play with her before going inside.

"I bet that dog's relieved to be outside," said a man talking to his friend.

"You can't take a dog inside a restaurant," the friend said. "Health regulations."

"I just meant, the dog's happy not to be on the menu! You know, Chinese food." They both laughed and walked away.

On the menu? For a split second, I thought he meant that Flurry should be the mascot of Kuai Le. But that didn't make sense, not with his tone of voice. Then I realized he meant something else. Something terrible.

"He's saying Flurry's glad we're not going to serve her as food," I said to Gwynn.

Gwynn looked at me, wide-eyed. I wrapped one arm

around Flurry and one arm around Gwynn and waited until the two men reached the end of the block. Then we ran inside to tell Mom what happened. Even though it was against the rules, we took Flurry with us, because now it didn't feel safe to leave her outside. Gwynn started crying as I told Mom what had happened.

"Why would someone say we would do that to Flurry? We love Flurry," Gwynn sobbed.

"It's an awful stereotype from a long time ago," said Mom, stroking Gwynn's hair. "It's an outrageous thing to say. It's racist. Are they still out there?"

"They just crossed the street," I said, pointing. "That way."

"Wait here," said Mom. She darted outside without even grabbing her coat. Gwynn and I also went outside, but we stayed by the door.

"Hey!" We watched Mom run down the street. The two men turned in surprise. "Those are my daughters, and that's my dog. I want you to say to me what you said in front of them." Mom marched right up to them and stood with her hands on her hips.

The man who had spoken first shoved his hands in his pockets. "We weren't talking to them," he said. "And I was just kidding about the dog."

"You made my daughter cry! A seven-year-old. Are you proud of yourself?"

Overheard

The man didn't say anything.

"Do you have a dog?" asked Mom.

He nodded, and Mom continued. "What makes you think we love our dog any less than you love yours? That was an awful, racist thing to say."

"We're not going to eat in your restaurant, dog or no dog," said the second man. He seemed mad that Mom was mad. "Because of the China virus."

"The proper term is COVID-19. Diseases start in lots of places," said Mom. "You don't mistreat the people who come from those places. And you don't say nasty things in front of children. Not if you're a functioning adult." She pointed her finger at them. "You said you wouldn't eat in my restaurant—good. Because you're not *allowed* in my restaurant." Then she turned on her heel and marched back to Gwynn and me. As soon as she reached us, we gave her hugs. Mom was shaking a little.

"You were so brave, Mom!" I said. "I wanted to say those things, but I couldn't find the words fast enough. You stopped them in their tracks."

"Bullies often stop when someone finally confronts them," said Mom. "But it's not your job to deal with adults like that."

"Is the restaurant going to be okay?" asked Gwynn.

"Of course!" said Mom. "We have good food, and

people will love it." She steered us toward the door. "Let's go inside. It's cold out here."

A moment later, Arne walked in. "Who's cold? I've got plenty of heat." He opened his big coat and wrapped it around Mom. "And what's Flurry doing in here?"

Mom leaned against Arne and sighed, while we filled Arne in. "This man walked by and made a joke that we were going to eat Flurry," I explained.

"And *then* Mom ran after them and yelled at them," said Gwynn.

"And then his friend said that he wouldn't eat here because of coronavirus. And Mom said he wasn't allowed in the restaurant," I added.

"Ooh," said Arne. "Then they got what they deserved, the wrath of your mom." He pretended to spit. "What ridiculous people. I don't like them."

Mom put her hand on her chest. "My heart is racing. I've never done anything like that. But I couldn't let those men talk in front of the girls that way. They needed to know their words matter."

Gwynn had stopped crying but her eyes were still red. "I don't like them either. Why would they be like that?"

"They are probably not even from here," said Arne. "They will go away, and poof! We will not have this problem. Believe me, honey. Don't cry, okay?" He put his arm around Gwynn. I hoped he wouldn't notice her necklace was gone.

"We did have a good day on the mountain," said Gwynn slowly. "Everybody wanted to try the zongzi." The two memories—one good, one bad—seemed to be fighting over what kind of day we were having.

"See? Nothing to worry about," Arne said. "Don't let those people bother you, okay?"

"It *does* bother me," I said, but not very loudly. "And people like that *do* live here."

"Let's not be upset," said Arne. "Your mother has been working so hard. I want to hear about the good part of your day. Tell me more about giving out the samples. Did people like them?"

Gwynn started telling Arne about our day on the mountain. Now she was smiling and laughing. Mom was happy to hear that the vegetarian zongzi were also popular. She hadn't been sure whether to put them on the menu.

I was glad to see them happy again. But underneath, Arne's comments bothered me almost as much as the men's. It felt like he was ignoring what had happened. As if he didn't even believe it was real.

Tricky Landing
Chapter 14

*T*he next day, Mom and I took Gwynn to her skating lesson. It was a teacher workday, which meant no school for us, so Gwynn got a lesson in the morning.

We watched Gwynn from the bleachers. "That waltz jump is looking good," said Mom. "I wonder if she'll be able to get a toe loop in for the competition."

"Ooh! She got—" Before I could finish my sentence, Gwynn slipped and fell on the ice. "She *almost* got it," I said, correcting myself.

"Margot says she really needs that toe loop," said Mom, who had been reading up on the rules for ice skating competitions. "I think it would be worse for her to have a program that's too easy than too hard." Mom checked the time. "We're going to have to get some lunch right after this. Gwynn is always so hungry after practice."

"A zongzi sounds good right about now," I said. My tummy rumbled in agreement. "Wait," I said. "What if you sold zongzi at the skating competition? They'd be a hit!"

Tricky Landing

Mom's eyes widened. "I love that idea," she declared. "We could make it a fundraiser for the ice skating club." She tapped her fingers. "What a brilliant idea, Cori. I'm going to find the rink manager. Wait here in case Gwynn finishes while I'm gone."

As Mom walked away, Gwynn tried the toe loop again. *C'mon Gwynn, you can do it!* I thought. This time she wobbled and waved her arms in the air but stayed on her feet. She was supposed to land on one foot, not two, but just staying upright was a start. She glanced over to where I was standing, and I gave her a thumbs-up. *Yes! You've got this!*

🌲🌲🌲

At school the next day, Cassidy asked me again when she could come see Flurry. "If I don't see her soon, she'll forget me!" said Cassidy. She tilted her head down and blinked at me, which is our friendship code for *You really can't resist me.* She handed me a sealed bag. "Look, I made Jake wear an old sweater for three days straight so you can use it for training. Even I can tell that it smells like him!"

Cassidy's helpfulness made me feel more guilty. I wished I'd just been up-front with her. "Thanks," I said. "I think I can use it pretty soon. Flurry is a really fast learner."

"So why don't I come over and help train her?" she

asked. "Or I could come by the restaurant again if it's easier to meet there."

"Things are really busy with Kuai Le," I said. "And my mom just—" I stopped myself. I'd nearly spilled the beans on Gwynn's skating competition. "Mom is, uh, going to sell her food at the rink this Saturday," I said. I tried to make it sound as dull as possible. "It's a publicity thing for the restaurant. We have to make a lot of food to sell." I didn't mention that it was also a fundraiser for the skating club, because then Cassidy would ask why Mom was fundraising for the skating club. Fortunately, I didn't have to say anything else, because our teacher called the class together.

"Let's calm down," said Mrs. Lomond over the chattering students. She had a trick to help us focus after lunch. "Smell the soup, breathe in through your nose. Cool the soup, breathe out through your mouth. Smell the soup, cool the soup." The class quieted down.

"Let's get out our history notebooks," Mrs. Lomond said.

After studying the Indigenous people of Colorado, we were now learning about the settlers who came here in the 1800s to find gold. It wasn't until 1876, the year of the hundredth birthday of the United States, that Colorado became a state. That's why one of Colorado's nicknames is the Centennial State.

Today we were looking at copies of old newspapers to

Tricky Landing

get a sense of what life was like in the nineteenth century. "Look at this," said a boy named Royce. "This place says it has dry goods. What are those?"

"Dry goods are things like cloth and thread," explained Mrs. Lomond. "Remember, pioneers and settlers made their own clothes, so they needed those supplies."

"I guess that's why this store is advertising 'ready made' clothes," Cassidy said, pointing at the paper.

"I think I might be related to the person who owned this business!" said Jenna. She pointed to an ad for Hively, Young & Company, which sold hardware and tinware. "My mom's maiden name is Hively."

"That would be something," said Mrs. Lomond. "You should ask your mother and let us know if you find out anything interesting."

A lot of the articles on the front page were just one or two sentences long. "Look at this," said Cassidy. She read the sentence out loud.
"'Alva Adams, of San Juan, took supper at the Junction

Wednesday evening.' *That's* news? Maybe a reporter should write about us eating dinner at your mom's restaurant, Cori."

A word caught my eye. "There's something about Chinese people here!" I said excitedly. Then I read the text more carefully.

———————◆———————

The Pacific coast is happy at last. If the cry that the "Chinese must go" did not prevail it at least gives them pleasure to say that "the Chinese must not come." 'Tis well.

———————◆———————

Even though the article used the words *happy, pleasure,* and *well,* it seemed like the things it was saying were not nice. I looked up at my teacher. "What does this mean?" I asked.

Mrs. Lomond tapped her lip. "I believe the article is talking about the Chinese Exclusion Act of 1882. That law prevented people from China from coming to the United States, and the Chinese people who were already here were not allowed to become citizens."

"What? I'm a citizen!" I said.

"The act is no longer in force," said Mrs. Lomond. She looked uncomfortable. "It was the first law to bar a specific group of people from coming into this country."

"Then why did that guy say, ''Tis well'? It's not well," said Cassidy. "It's terrible."

"I'm afraid a lot of people felt hostile toward Chinese people back then," said Mrs. Lomond. "They didn't want them to come work in the mines and compete for jobs."

A boy named Bryce raised his hand. "My grandpa said that a town nearby used to have a sign saying 'All China-men will be shot.'" Bryce lowered his head. "Sorry. That sounds mean."

"It *is* mean—thank you for pointing that out," said Mrs. Lomond. "But these are things we should know. It's part of our history that doesn't get talked about enough. The important thing," she added, "is to learn from the past so we don't make the same mistakes."

I nodded. In a weird way, I was glad to know the truth, even if it was ugly and hurtful.

Now I wanted to tell Arne what I had learned. Maybe knowing that history would help him understand what had been happening to me.

🌲🌲🌲

When I got home from school, I took Flurry outside to pee, and then we worked on her training. We had gotten her a teal harness from the pet store, and she knew that putting it on meant it was time to practice her skills. Flurry was getting really good at "stay" while I hid behind a tree or under the patio table. I came close to successfully hiding from her once, when I went behind some trees and hid behind a stack of firewood. From where I was crouched down, I could see Flurry walk straight past me toward the fence.

I thought I had her fooled, but Flurry suddenly snapped her head back. I tried not to make a sound, but that didn't keep me hidden. A black nose appeared by my hand.

"You found me!" I said. She had found my scent. As a reward, we played tug-of-war with the tug toy I'd brought. "Good girl!"

Gwynn came outside and watched us. "I wish *I* could go hide," she said.

I was about to invite her to hide to help train Flurry, but then I realized that wasn't what she meant.

"I can't land the toe loop at all!" she moaned. "I just

fall and fall about a million times. I don't even want to go to my lesson."

"You'll get it," I said. "I saw you yesterday. You were soooo close."

"I was?" said Gwynn. "I don't remember that."

"Sure! Mom and I were watching you work on your toe loop. I sent you a sister brain at that moment. I thought, *C'mon Gwynn, you can do it!* And you landed on your feet." I tried not to smile when I said "sister brain," because Gwynn took it so seriously.

Her face lit up. "I think I felt that! But I'm supposed to land on one foot," Gwynn pointed out.

"You're going to get it," I said. "You just have to keep practicing. Don't give up."

"I think I'll need sister brain during the competition," said Gwynn. "Especially right at that moment when I do the toe loop."

"We're all going to be there," I said. "Mom, Dad, Arne, and me. The only one who isn't coming is Flurry."

Gwynn squeezed my hand. "But you're the only one who can do sister brain!"

"I'll be there with sister brain," I promised. "I can't imagine where else I would want to be."

🌲🌲

Corinne

That night, Arne brought home takeout food because Mom had been working so hard at the restaurant, making extra food for Gwynn's skating competition. He passed around tacos, rice and beans, and salad.

"I thought that having a chef for a wife meant I'd never have to get takeout," said Arne, joking.

"Having a chef for a wife means you always have to get takeout," teased Mom.

"Dad says when you do the same things on vacation as you do at work, it's called a busman's holiday," I said. Then I put my hand over my mouth. I'd broken my own rule about not mentioning Dad in front of Arne, and vice versa. I hoped Mom and Arne weren't mad.

"Your dad is a very knowledgeable guy," said Arne. "I can see you girls learn a lot from him."

I changed the subject. "These tacos are really good."

"It's not even Tuesday!" said Gwynn. Arne looked confused, so I explained that at school we had Taco Tuesdays.

"So what else is happening at school?" asked Arne. "Is there anything I should put on my calendar?"

"We're having a concert in two weeks," said Gwynn. "You can come if you want."

"Of course I want!" said Arne. "But I don't always get what I want. I think I am away that week. Big business." He took out his phone.

Tricky Landing

"No phones at the table," Mom reminded him.

Arne frowned. "But I'm checking my calendar." My stomach tightened. Were they fighting?

Just then, Flurry ran in with one of Arne's shoes in her mouth. "No, Flurry!" shouted Arne. "That's one of my new shoes."

I jumped up from the table, took the shoe away from Flurry, and told her no. Arne has really nice shoes. This one was soft brown leather. I gave Flurry a rawhide bone to chew on. "You don't need to shout at her," I said. "We just have to train her properly." I put my arm around Flurry.

Arne took a deep breath. "Yes, you're right. I'm sorry. But I don't want that dog to ruin my shoes." I did not like the way Arne said "that dog."

"Let's all calm down," said Mom. "Arne, if Flurry has gotten one of your shoes, then the shoes weren't put away in the right place. I thought we agreed on the garage." Arne nodded. "Okay, let's talk about something else. Did anything interesting happen at school today?" Mom asked this question all the time, but today I actually did have something interesting to mention: the Chinese Exclusion Act.

"We had a substitute teacher," said Gwynn.

Arne's phone rang. He glanced down at the screen. "I've got to take this," he said as he got up from the table. He went to the living room and started speaking in Swedish.

Corinne

Mom passed me the beans and rice. "You can tell Gwynn and me what happened at school today," she said.

"But I really wanted Arne to hear, too," I said, staring at his back. Couldn't Arne tell that I was about to tell him something important? Too bad there wasn't such a thing as stepfather brain.

Broken Promise

Chapter 15

On the morning of Gwynn's competition, she woke me up. At 5:00 a.m.

"Cori," she whispered. I felt a poke at my feet.

I moaned. "It's still dark."

"I know," she said. "But I was too excited to sleep. Look." We were both whispering because Flurry was in our room, too, still sleeping.

I opened one eye and saw Gwynn standing on the ladder to my bed. I could see her from the waist up. "Ooh, Gwynn, you are so beautiful," I said. I sat up and rubbed my eyes so I could get a better look.

Gwynn was wearing a pale purple dress that made her skin light up. Pink flowers crept over one shoulder and down the bodice. The whole dress sparkled, but not as much as Gwynn. She had the biggest smile on her face, and her eyes were shining.

"Do you ever feel like you're about to do something really big?" asked Gwynn. "Because I feel like that now."

"I feel like that when I teach Flurry something new," I said. "When I can see that she gets it and really understands me, it's huge."

"I keep telling myself that my nervous feelings are really excited feelings," said Gwynn. "That way I don't feel so scared." She let out a long, slow breath. "Ms. Margot said I shouldn't wear jewelry, but I wish I had my necklace with me. Just to bring as a good luck charm."

"You can bring mine," I offered. I kept mine in the black velvet box that it came in.

"It's not the same," said Gwynn. She sighed. "It's okay. We'll go get it soon, when we go back to the shrine."

"That's right. And you'll be great," I told her. "With sister brain, you can't be stopped." I yawned. "But it would be good if we could sleep a little longer."

"Can I sleep up here with you?" asked Gwynn. "I'll lie very still because I don't want to wrinkle my costume."

I scooted over so that Gwynn could climb in between me and the wall. Gwynn lay flat on her back and closed her eyes. "I'm going to dream about my routine," she announced.

🌲🌲🌲

We drove to the rink after lunch. We could have walked there from Arne's house, but Mom had lots of trays of food to sell today. After Gwynn was checked in, Arne and I helped Mom bring everything inside.

"Is that for me?" asked one of the moms cheerfully. "Smells good!"

"We'll have the table set up in a few minutes. Come on by," said Mom. She was wearing her business-lady face, which meant that she was being extra bright and bubbly. "Buy lots! It's a fundraiser for the skating club."

We wiped down the table and then set out the trays of food. One tray had the zongzi with meat, and one tray had vegetarian. Two other trays had neat rows of dumplings. Mom also set up a burner to make *cong you bing*.

"Looks good!" Dad stopped by and admired the table. He had also come to watch Gwynn skate. "You'll be sold out in ten minutes."

"I have more trays," said Mom. "But I'd love to sell out."

They were both smiling and being nice to each other, which was the best feeling. I wasn't sure whether I should sit with Dad or with Mom and Arne during the competition, but for now we were all hanging out together.

"I saw a T-shirt stand," said Arne. "Do you want to go pick out a T-shirt for Gwynn? Do you want one?" He pulled out his wallet and handed me two twenties.

I told him that I didn't need one but that I would get one for Gwynn. I walked over to the T-shirt stand and looked at the different styles. I decided to get a blue T-shirt that had the name of the competition on it, and I could get Gwynn's name printed on the back.

"Chinese flu! Coming through!" I turned around and saw the boy with the jagged bangs. He was covering his mouth and laughing at me. He had two friends with him and they were all carrying hockey bags. One friend laughed half-heartedly. The other one stayed silent.

I thought about my mom when she had stood up to the two men. I forced myself to look straight at the boy. "Why do you keep saying that?" I asked him. "It's really mean, and it's not clever at all." I took a deep breath. "It's racist, if you want to know the truth."

Broken Promise

"She's right. You should be ashamed of yourself," said the T-shirt seller to the boy. She looked like she was in high school. Maybe she was one of the older skaters. "That's not what we're about here." She handed me my change and gave my hand a little squeeze. I let out a breath I didn't realize I'd been holding.

The boy stood there with his mouth open. Then one of his friends gave him a push to keep walking. That boy mouthed *Sorry* to me.

I walked back to where Arne was standing and handed him his change. "What's the matter?" asked Arne. Dad was gone, and Mom was busy selling food to a line of hungry people. I looked down and saw my hands were trembling. My heart was still pounding. I felt like I had just run a mile.

I pointed to the T-shirt stand. "It's that boy again. The one I saw here the first day Gwynn had practice. He made a racist comment to me. But this time I told him to knock it off." I was proud of myself and a little scared, all at the same time. Had I really just done that?

"What?" Arne took the change and put it in his pocket, frowning. "Corinne, what are you talking about? What boy?"

"The one who called me kung flu! Remember? I told you about it."

"Ah, that boy." Arne nodded. "Yes, I remember now. His parents need to teach that boy some manners."

"Not just manners," I said. "Like, how to be a decent human being."

"Then again," said Arne, "the parents are where many children learn those ideas."

"That's why I spoke up," I said tightly. "Mom showed me how to do it. And the girl at the T-shirt stand backed me up." I wanted Arne to say something about what I had done, how brave and right I had been.

"So true! Your mother, what a wonder," said Arne. He put his arm around me. "Look, forget about him. We need to help your mother with the food, okay? Not focus on those idiots." He shook his head. "This is Gwynn's day. We have to support her. If we talk about that boy, it's like letting him win."

Smell the soup, breathe in. Cool the soup, breathe out. Smell the soup, cool the soup. *I don't want to let him win either,* I thought. *Of course I want to support Gwynn.* But couldn't Arne support *me,* too?

I was considering how to tell Arne this when the announcer said that everyone should take their seats. Gwynn was in Level 1, which would be going first. Ms. Margot had explained that within each level, the skaters were put in groups of six and everyone got a medal. I hoped Gwynn wasn't scared. I found Dad in the bleachers, and together we watched the first group of skaters compete. Some of them looked nervous.

"Gwynn's up next," Dad whispered to me. I sat up straighter and got ready to send sister brain to her.

When the announcer said Gwynn's name, Dad and I cheered. She didn't look scared as she glided onto the ice. She gazed out into the audience and smiled as the first notes of the song "Happy" began to play. The song matched her mood. Gwynn hopped up and began skating around the rink.

"Cori!" Someone was shout-whispering my name. I looked around and spotted Cassidy at the end of my row. She looked shocked. Suddenly my stomach felt as if I had swallowed a ball of ice.

I got up and made my way to her. "What are you doing here?" I asked.

"I came by to check out your mom's food table." Cassidy jabbed her finger toward the ice. "And your mom said that Gwynn was skating!"

I turned away from Cassidy to watch Gwynn land a perfect waltz jump.

"Why didn't you tell me?" hissed Cassidy.

I didn't know how to answer. "I was going to!" I whispered back. I kept one eye on the ice. "I've been busy." I felt uncomfortable standing in the aisle. I knew it was rude to the people behind us.

"Is this what you were doing every time you said you were too busy to hang out with me? Taking Gwynn to skating practice?" asked Cassidy. She sounded equally hurt and angry. "And all this time, you kept talking about going to the dentist." People nearby sent annoyed glances my way, as if they were upset with me, too.

"I did go to the dentist," I said. "Once." My words sounded hollow. My throat tightened. I glanced over at the ice. Gwynn's toe loop was coming up.

"But you never, ever mentioned Gwynn taking skating lessons!" said Cassidy. "Not even when we watched the skating competition at your mom's restaurant. You could have told me then."

I nodded numbly. I couldn't look at her.

"You kept this a secret on purpose. You lied to me!" Cassidy glared at me, her eyes watering. I had hurt her in the worst way.

"I didn't mean to!" I cried. The words came bursting out, as if to get the awful, heavy feeling off my chest. The crowd gasped, not just at my shouting, but at its effect on Gwynn. Just as she landed her toe loop, she stumbled and went sprawling across the ice.

Gwynn raised her head, looking just as betrayed and hurt as Cassidy. I hadn't sent her sister brain. I had made things worse.

Broken Promise

Mom appeared and grabbed my arm. She must have seen everything from the food table and come running. "What is going on, Corinne?"

Dad scooted down the row and into the aisle. *Mei-Ling Tan! What were you thinking?* Dad was speaking in Chinese, but anyone could tell from his tone that he was mad.

Arne appeared next to Mom. He folded his arms and frowned.

"I'm sorry," I pleaded. "I'm sorry." I didn't even know who I was saying it to. Maybe I was apologizing to everyone. Cassidy, Gwynn, Mom, Dad, Arne. The crowd. Then I ran out of the rink.

A Cold, Dark Night

Chapter 16

I ran down the street—away from the rink, away from all the people I had disappointed. The cold air whipped my face. I ran until my lungs burned, and then I bent forward, trying to catch my breath between sobs. I couldn't run fast enough to get away from my feelings.

I looked around. Where could I go? Arne's house was locked. The restaurant was, too. I checked my phone for the bus schedule. I could take the bus to Dad's house, but I'd have to wait an hour for it to come. My phone battery was down to five percent. The cold air at the rink must have used up a lot of power.

Then I looked up at the mountains and realized exactly where I should go. *Ajax.* I would go to the sister shrine and get Gwynn's necklace as a way of making things up to her. It wouldn't fix everything, but it would be a start. Maybe I'd also think of a way to make things right with Cassidy.

I jogged over to the gondola and flashed my pass. The operator frowned. "You're alone? And where are your skis?"

A Cold, Dark Night

I looked at my hands, fumbling for an excuse. I was still holding Gwynn's competition T-shirt. "I'm meeting my family at Sundeck," I said, trying to sound confident. The operator nodded and let me board.

I got a gondola to myself. Aspen slowly became smaller and smaller and then disappeared, leaving only the trees and the mountains in view. The only sounds I could hear were the hum of the gondola motor and my own breathing.

At the top, I retraced the path Gwynn and I had taken when we handed out the zongzi samples. That day, we had made our way to Spar Gulch to get back into town. The sister shrine was between two of the trails coming down from the eastern side of the gulch, but the landscape looked different walking down the mountain than it did when we had skied down it. The snow crunched under my feet. They were getting cold. I was wearing fuzzy boots and leggings. I had dressed for being at an ice rink, not on the mountain. I scrunched down in my jacket, trying to stay warm. I stuck to the side of the trail, out of the way of the skiers whooshing down the mountain.

As I walked, I kept hearing Mom, Dad, Arne, and Cassidy in my head. Their disappointment and confusion. "You lied to me!" echoed in my ears. Then I pictured Gwynn as she looked up from the ice, shocked that she had fallen, maybe more surprised that I had let her down.

I walked faster, to get away from the angry voices and sad faces in my head.

Finally, I spotted a horseshoe of trees. The shrine! I began walking toward it, stumbling as the cold crept up my legs.

I peered at the branch where the shrine should have been. Where were our Seven Sisters pinecones? Where was Gwynn's necklace, her scrunchie, the tag from the zongzi? Maybe they were buried under the snow. I gently brushed the snow off the branch, trying to make sure I didn't knock the items to the ground.

Nothing. Nothing but snow and branches. I was in the wrong place.

A stiff wind was starting up as I turned to go back toward the trail. I expected the wide expanse of the ski trail to pop into view after a bit of walking, but it didn't. I kept going. The trail should have appeared by now. Finally, I stopped and stared into the woods around me, looking for a clue, something that would show me the right way back, but everything that seemed familiar had disappeared.

What had I done? I felt my heart shrink inside my chest. My heart knew before my brain grasped the truth: I was lost.

Finding a Way Home
Chapter 17

My first instinct was to start running again. No, that was stupid. I took a deep breath and tried to think. My phone was completely dead. I had to stay put. I had to stay warm. That was what Zach had said. I just never thought his advice would apply to me. I was supposed to be the rescuer, not the person who was lost. Even the tears on my face felt cold. *Not now,* I told myself. *Stop crying. Stay calm. Smell the soup, cool the soup. Smell the soup, cool the soup.*

Think. I took a quick inventory of what I had. I wrapped Gwynn's T-shirt around my neck like a scarf. I clapped my hands together and stomped my feet to keep my circulation going. I found a plastic bag in my pocket for picking up after Flurry—it could help keep me dry.

And now, I had to stay here. I noticed that one of the evergreens had a deep hollow between its roots. I scooped out the snow down to the ground. Then I dragged over some boughs and leaned them against the tree, over the hole. They would protect me from the falling snow. I smoothed out the bag on the ground so I could sit on it, and then I tucked myself into the hole. I felt a tiny bit warmer, now that the wind wasn't blowing on me. Sunset was coming, which meant the mountain would only get colder.

Would someone find me? Would my family think to look here? I had to hope.

Suddenly I remembered the other important job I had. I needed to make noise so someone could find me.

"I'M HERE!"

"I'M HERE!"

"I'M HERE!"

Building the shelter had warmed me up and given me something to do, but now I had to wait. I knew I could be waiting for a long time.

I thought of my favorite warm things. Flannel sheets. A mug of hot chocolate. A day on the river under the hot summer sun. Making *huo guo* with my family, with the steam rising up in our faces as we cooked slices of beef and pork in a big pot of broth. I loved the last step of *huo guo,* when we added noodles and vegetables and made soup. My stomach rumbled. Being out in the cold made me hungrier, and thinking of food wasn't helping.

"I'M HERE!" I had to keep calling out, even though it seemed pointless and my throat was getting raw. I wished I had a whistle with me.

Finding a Way Home

I looked at the trees, trying to identify them in the waning light. I thought I could make out the silhouette of a skinny lodgepole pine against the sky, but I wasn't sure. The mountain was a kind of home to me—especially the sister shrine. It was our special place in the world, mine and Gwynn's. But now it was different. I was alone. Now I realized that home is more than a place—it's people. The Chinese character *jia* could mean home, but it could also mean family.

Home was with Mom and Gwynn. And Dad. Flurry. And even Arne. The more I thought about the people I loved, the more I began to worry that I wouldn't see them again. What if I never saw Gwynn land her toe loop, or never got to show Cassidy my new room? I wanted to apologize and make things right, no matter what. I wanted a chance to talk to Arne about what I'd learned. I wanted to see Kuai Le open and have lines out the door to eat Mom's good food. I wanted Dad to teach me how to do more tricks like Eileen Gu and show me more stars.

"I'M HERE!" I'm ready to be found. To come home. To make amends. To do better. *You just have to find me.* My voice was getting weaker. I wondered how many more times I could scream.

I looked up at the night sky and spotted the Pleiades. The Seven Sisters. Sisters could do anything together. How many times had Gwynn and I figured that out? We had survived our parents' divorce and moving and so many other things because we had each other. But what was I supposed to do without her—and what would she do without me? I swallowed hard. No, nothing was going to happen to me. I was going to survive. I had to stay warm. I could not give up. I tucked my hands into my armpits. The cold was making me feel sleepy and dumb. I just wanted to close my eyes for a few minutes.

At that moment, the wind stopped blowing and the air became perfectly still. I heard the crunch of snow breaking and a heavy breath. *Whuff.*

Suddenly I wasn't sleepy anymore. I swallowed. Bears made that sound. Bears lumbered around, sniffing for food. They were always hungry.

I knew I was supposed to make myself big to scare away a bear. But the thought of crawling out of the shelter terrified me. I curled myself into a tight ball, trying to work up the courage to spring out of the hole. *On the count of three*, I told myself. *One . . . two . . .*

Teeth gripped my jacket, jerking my arm up. The bear! The bear had found me, and it was dragging me out of my hole. I screamed.

And looked right into Flurry's eyes.

Flurry? Flurry barked and wagged her tail. I tried to

stand and almost fell back into the hole. My legs shook, numb with cold as relief flooded my body. It wasn't a bear. It was Flurry! And if Flurry was here, then maybe people were coming. Flurry pawed at me. To her, this was just another game of hide-and-seek. Then I remembered that I was supposed to reward Flurry for finding me.

"You found me!" I scratched behind her ears. "Good girl!" She barked and tugged on my sleeve. "I'm not quite up for tug-of-war, though." I tried to make my voice bright and happy, but my throat was raspy from yelling.

I needed to call out again. "I'M HERE!" I screamed as loud as I could.

This time, a voice shouted back. "Corinne?!"

🌲🌲🌲

A ski patroller named Gary pulled me down the mountain on a toboggan. He explained that it would be the fastest and safest way to get me down. I had always wondered what it was like to lie flat in the toboggan like that, if it would be scary to be so close to the ground with the patroller's skis right by your face. But as we whooshed down the mountain, as tiny sprays of snow flew over me, the toboggan thumped and turned, and the sky loomed large and dark overhead, I realized that as long as I was going back to my family, I didn't care about anything else.

Corinne

At the bottom of the mountain, the ski patrollers carried me into the back of a lodge. Flurry followed us. Patrol members were walking around, talking. Some stopped to pet Flurry and tell her what a good girl she was. I was still shivering. As soon as she saw me, Mom wrapped a blanket around me and held me very, very tightly.

"Corinne." Her voice broke. She just said my name. "Corinne." I buried my face in her shoulder and took a deep breath, smelling the things that made her my mom. Dad and Gwynn joined us, and for a moment, we were a tight circle, the way our family used to be.

Dad handed me a cup of warm apple cider. "This will help warm you up."

"Is Flurry okay?" I asked. I looked around the room until I spotted her. One of the ski patrollers was toweling her off. I didn't want to let her out of my sight.

"How did you know where to look?" I asked, thinking of the moment when Flurry's face appeared.

"Gwynn thought you might go to the sister shrine," said Mom. "Since you could get to the gondola on foot, Arne had them check the system for your pass. And Dad notified the ski patrol."

"The sister shrine must be new," said Dad. "I've never heard of it."

"We made it," Gwynn told him. "We got the idea after

seeing the Calvin and Hobbes shrine."

"I couldn't find it," I said. "I got confused." Tears sprang into my eyes. I still hadn't made things right for Gwynn. I reached out and held her hand. "I'm sorry. I don't know if we'll be able to find your necklace."

Gwynn was not bothered. "We'll find it," she said. "We just need to be together."

Gary joined us. "You were gone for almost four hours in the cold," Gary told me. "Bet it felt longer to your parents."

Mom shook her head. Her eyes were red from crying. "Every minute you were gone seemed like an eternity. I felt like we couldn't move fast enough."

"Glad we found you when we did," Gary said. "You did a good job, making a shelter and, of course, that yell. People sometimes forget to keep yelling." He patted me on the shoulder. "Good job."

"It was my idea to get Flurry," said Gwynn. She had attached herself to my side, and we'd called Flurry to jump into our laps. "And Flurry's vest. I thought that even though Flurry isn't an official search and rescue dog, she would know how to look for you. I put on her vest and told her to search."

"Flurry did an amazing job," said Mom. She scratched Flurry under her chin, one of her favorite places. "This doggy has some gourmet meals in her future!"

Finding a Way Home

"Did you get my sister brain messages?" asked Gwynn. "I kept telling you not to give up."

Gwynn's question made me wonder. Had I gotten a sister brain message? That moment when I thought I might give up, but then I realized I needed to hang on—maybe that was Gwynn. Or maybe sister brain was just another way of saying *I love you*.

"Promise me you won't do that again," said Mom. "Running away does not solve problems."

"I felt so terrible," I said. "I was trying to fix things. To make up for what I did."

"There's no problem so big that we can't fix it together," said Mom. "And there's nothing you can do that would make us not love you, okay?"

We sat in the lodge as volunteers began to check back in. Dad's coworkers had come out to help search, and he thanked them for their help.

Arne came in and just stared at me for a minute. His eyes were red-rimmed like Mom's—he'd been crying. He held out his arms, and I went to him in a hug.

"Corinne," he said. His voice was choked up. "I was on the top of the mountain when I got the call that you'd been found. I was ready to outrun the gondola down here."

"I'm okay," I told him. "I'm cold, but I'm okay."

"I've never been so frightened in my life," Arne said.

Corinne

I thought of Arne's fear of heights. "How did you get to the top of the mountain?"

"I took the gondola, of course," said Arne. "It's the fastest way. And then I took it back down."

"I thought you never rode the gondola," I said. "Because of your acrophobia."

"This is the one exception," said Arne. "For you. Because I was more scared of losing you than riding the gondola."

Arne had taken the gondola. For me.

Arne lowered his head. "While I was looking for you, I started thinking about our last conversation. I played it like a recording in my head. I thought about how I always tried to keep you from feeling sad or angry when something bad happened. I just want you to be happy. But you weren't happy anyway, and then you ran off."

I knotted my fingers into Flurry's fur. Part of me wanted to talk about only good things right now, but wasn't that the problem? I took a deep breath. "You don't have to try to make me happy all the time. More than anything, I want you to listen and believe me."

Arne was silent for a moment. He just nodded and took it in. "Yes," he said. "I will try. I promise." We hugged again.

Then Arne walked over to Dad and stuck out his hand. "Thank goodness you called the ski patrol so quickly," Arne said to him.

Finding a Way Home

Dad shook Arne's hand. "Good idea to check for Corinne's ski pass," said Dad. For a moment it seemed as if that was all they were going to say. But then Dad added, "You love my girls," and he clapped his free hand over their clasped ones. It wasn't a question. It was a statement.

"Of course," said Arne. He seemed surprised. "Of course." Mom came over and stood near them. She looked at Dad and then looked at Arne, just listening.

Something inside Dad seemed to loosen. "Then they are lucky to have you," he said.

"They are lucky to have all of us," said Arne. "And we are lucky to have them."

It was such a small shift, but then I understood. I could talk to Dad about Arne because we were together, even if we lived in different houses. They had always said it was okay, but now I could see for myself that it was. That this was the shape of our new family.

🌲🌲🌲

"I can't believe you thought we weren't going to be friends," said Cassidy, "because of *ice skating*." Cassidy had come over the next day, and Gwynn and I were showing her our room. Normally I'd feel annoyed if Gwynn stuck around when Cassidy came over, but now it was nice. Gwynn showed Cassidy how the fireplace worked. You just flicked a switch and the fire came on.

"You were pretty mad," I said. "About Gwynn's skating."

"I was mad that you *lied* about Gwynn skating, not that she was skating," said Cassidy. "There's a difference."

"You said you didn't like girls who skate competitively. You said they were snobs. I was afraid you would think Gwynn and I were snobs if Gwynn was one of those girls," I said.

Cassidy shrugged. "Looks like I might be wrong. Maybe you were meant to change my mind."

I thought of the boy with the jagged bangs. Maybe he would change his mind. Maybe his friend who had mouthed *Sorry* to me would help him do it.

"Will you come to my next competition?" Gwynn asked Cassidy. "On purpose this time?"

"Naturally," said Cassidy. "And I already have ideas for your next costume."

Cassidy and Gwynn got out some paper and colored pencils and started sketching costume ideas. But I wasn't quite ready to let go of what I had done. What had Gwynn said about the shrine that day on the mountain? *It doesn't feel special enough.* This was sort of the same thing. I hadn't made things right enough yet.

"I was *going* to tell you," I told Cassidy. "That was my plan. I kept thinking that if I waited, it would be easier. But then it kind of snowballed, and I didn't know where to start."

She nodded. "I know."

"Cassidy," I said, "I'm sorry. I really am. You're the best friend I've ever had, and I was afraid that we would stop being friends. And if that had happened, it would have been all my fault."

"Cori," said Cassidy. She lifted her head and looked at me. "I forgive you." And those words, they felt so good. "It's going to take a lot more than a fancy bedroom and a sister who ice skates to break us up. We can figure out pretty much anything, as long as we put our minds to it."

Cassidy plopped down into the ski chair and looked around the room. "Hey, I have an idea of where you can put your Eileen Gu poster without messing up the"—she waved her arms around—"fanciness."

"Where?" I asked. Having to hang the poster in our closet still bothered me.

"You can put it on the back of your door. That way, you can see it when the door is closed, but to everyone else, the room looks the same."

"That's it!" We high-fived. Flurry barked in support. "You're incredible!" I told her.

"You would have thought of it, too," said Cassidy. "You just needed time to think about it."

"There's always a solution," I said. And not just for

figuring out where to hang your posters. I had discovered that being honest and forgiving each other could solve pretty much any relationship problem.

"Maybe Mom will let us make s'mores in the fireplace!" said Gwynn. She ran into the hallway, yelling for Mom.

"Maybe we can ask your mom if we can have a sleepover," suggested Cassidy.

"Here or at your house?" I asked.

Cassidy shrugged. "I was thinking here, but either way is fine."

I paused. Having a sleepover here was a way of making it official. This wasn't just Arne's house anymore. It was our house.

"Let's ask if you can stay here," I said. "It'd be nice to stay home tonight."

Ski Sisters

Sisters Kaya and Marley, ages fourteen and twelve, have been skiing together since they were toddlers. Now they're learning mountain safety and first aid skills through SheJumps, an organization that helps girls get involved in outdoor activities. The sisters have practiced skills like caring for injured skiers, exiting a chairlift during an emergency, and talking on walkie-talkies using ski patrol lingo. They've even gotten to tow a rescue toboggan down the mountain—and ride inside!

"Riding in the toboggan is a little uncomfortable," Kaya says, "but you feel safe because the ski patroller towing you knows what they're doing."

"I hope that's the only time I'll have to ride in one," Marley says. "But it was fun!"

Kaya lies flat on a rescue backboard before being lifted into a toboggan.

One thing Kaya and Marley love is meeting avalanche rescue dogs. Sometimes they get to ride with a dog in the ski lift or help the dogs search for scents in the snow.

"One time, someone slept with a sweater for a whole week," Marley explains. "Then they hid it in the snow, and the dog had to go find it." It was important for the girls to be very quiet, so the dog could focus on the search.

"The dogs are very respectful and sweet," Kaya adds. "It's cool to see them in action, helping someone on the mountain, riding up a chairlift, or going down a ski run."

These dogs are ready for a rescue!

The girls don't have a dog of their own to train, but they've been asking for one!

One of the best things about SheJumps is spending time with other girls who have the same interests. "It feels like a big family," Kaya says. "You can just be yourself!"

Even when junior ski patrol training covers serious topics, the sisters make it fun. Once, Kaya and Marley got to pretend to be injured skiers who had fallen from a chairlift. They loved putting on makeup and fake blood, and practicing their acting skills.

"We were supposed to cry and scream," Kaya adds. "It was pretty intense."

As part of an exercise, ski patrollers assessed the girls' "injuries" and triaged them based on how serious their conditions were. Kaya's group won T-shirts for their excellent acting abilities!

Top: Marley pretends to have a broken leg.

Bottom: Kaya uses a compass to find her location.

Though Kaya and Marley have never gotten hurt on the mountain, their training has still come in handy. Once, the girls were skiing down their last run of the day with their grandpa. But when Kaya got to the bottom, Marley was gone!

"I got lost," Marley says. Luckily, her ski patrol instructors had given her an emergency contact card that she kept in her coat pocket when skiing. "I stayed where I was and asked an adult for help." The adult used the card to call Marley's grandpa, and soon the family was reunited.

For any girls interested in trying a new outdoor sport like skiing, Marley and Kaya have some advice.

"Get up on the mountain, and then you can decide whether you like it," Marley says. "Don't decide you can't do it before you've even tried!"

"Just do it!" Kaya says. "You're going to be happy you had the experience."

We're on top of the world!

Life with Zoe

While author Wendy Wan-Long Shang wrote Corinne's story, she was training a puppy at home, too! It all started in early 2020, when Wendy's fifteen-year-old daughter, Kate, decided that life during the pandemic would be more fun with a dog. Thanks to Kate's persistence, a rescued black Lab mix soon joined the family! Here, Kate gives a glimpse into life with Zoe.

How did you first meet Zoe?

We went to meet the puppies when they were six weeks old. The foster mom put them in a huge pen on her front porch, and we got to go inside. They were very sleepy. We decided to get the puppy that the foster mom described as "the smart one."

How did you choose her name?

We went through several rounds of voting and brainstorming. My brothers and I made a pitch for combining Zoe and Frog, just because we thought it was funny, but my parents vetoed it. Our veterinarian is a family friend, though, so she wrote "Zoeyfrog" in the office record!

What do you and Zoe like to do together?

I like to chase her around the house. Zoe loves being chased! We also have a game where we make her sit and stay while we hide one of her toys, and then she has to find it.

Zoe loves playing with my cousin's dog, who lives next door. She'll stand at the gate between our backyards like a person and cry for her to play! I also love these long grunting noises that Zoe makes. We call her a moo-cow when she does that.

Does Zoe ever get into mischief?

Recently, we couldn't figure out why someone was leaving the sliding door open. My mom even blamed me. Then we realized that Zoe had figured out how to push open the door! We tried being more careful about locking the door, but she quickly figured that out, too! Living with Zoe means trying to stay one step ahead.

MEET AUTHOR
Wendy Wan-Long Shang

Wendy's favorite things are freshly sharpened pencils, dogs, quiet mornings, good books, and the Spelling Bee puzzle in the *New York Times*. She wishes she were good at knitting and tennis, but has not quite devoted enough time to either endeavor . . . yet. Wendy writes about different aspects of the Chinese American experience through her middle-grade and picture books. She also wrote the novel adaptation of the Netflix original *Over the Moon*. Wendy works on race and justice issues for the Pretrial Justice Institute. She lives with her family in Falls Church, Virginia.

MEET ILLUSTRATOR
Peijin Yang

Peijin is a freelance illustrator who was born and raised in Tianjin, China, and now lives in Munich, Germany. She discovered her love for painting after college and started her art journey in 2017. Since then she has been creating illustrations for book publishers and working for clients all over the world. Her personal artworks are also very popular and widely shared on social media.